MERMAIDS

Mermaids

Short Stories
by
ANA VIDOSAVLJEVIC

Adelaide Books
New York / Lisbon
2020

MERMAIDS
Short Stories
By Ana Vidosavljevic

Copyright © by Ana Vidosavljevic
Cover design © 2020 Adelaide Books

Published by Adelaide Books, New York / Lisbon
adelaidebooks.org

Editor-in-Chief
Stevan V. Nikolic

For any information, please address Adelaide Books
at info@adelaidebooks.org or write to:
Adelaide Books
244 Fifth Ave. Suite D27
New York, NY, 10001

ISBN: 978-1-951214-48-7
Printed in the United States of America

Contents

IT'S A KIND OF MAGIC

THE WORLD WE KNOW

A Recurring Dream

Mila woke up to the sound of Fajr prayer[1]. It was still pitch-dark outside. She came close to the window and pulled back the curtain. The sky was overloaded with starts. Mila was gazing at the beautiful twinkling carpet above. It was stunning. It seemed so close, as though she could reach and touch it. As though she could hold the moon in her hand. She lowered her head and she saw man hurrying to the mosque. She loved listening the early morning prayer. It was full of sorrow, lament, mystery and artistic beauty at the same time. She couldn't wait the dawn and she was eager not only to walk the streets of Sanliurfa[2], but to visit Gobekli Tepe[3] as well. For most of people, laymen, Gobekli Tepe was an archaeological site. For archaeologists, anthropologists and those who studied human life and human culture this was an exquisite place, a place which seemed to not only question certain religious beliefs but whose mysterious stones maybe marked the site of the Garden of Eden[4].

---

[1] The first of the five daily prayers recited by practicing Muslims.

[2] A city in south-eastern Turkey.

[3] An archaeological site dating from roughly 12000 years ago. It is believed that Gobekli Tepe is the first temple of the world.

[4] Or (often) Paradise is the biblical "garden of God".

Mila was not an archaeologist or anthropologist and she had never before been to Gobekli Tepe. However, a year ago, she had met a young archaeologist who had told her the stories and legends about this mysterious place. And her interest for this place grew so much that she started dreaming it. Those dreams were so vivid and so puzzling that they colored her everyday life. Not a day passed without her thinking about this place. Often would she dream the Gobekli Tepe's hills, yellow dust and strange skulls that were half-human and half-animal. Those dreams didn't let her do anything else except read about Gobekli Tepe. And the more she read about it, the more intense her desire to visit it became.

One dream especially kept her anxious and restless. She was sleeping but she was tired. That recurring dream exhausted her. Mila dreamed that she was walking alone on a dusty road that led to Gobekli Tepe. The sun was at its zenith and the burning ground was throwing out the golden dust.

Those golden clouds blurred her vision. But still, she could anticipate something strange approaching her. It was not a man, nor a bird and it didn't seem like any animal either. And still, it seemed alive. Alive but not walking, flying or slithering. It was more floating through the hot air.

The closer it was, the stronger her heart was beating. When it was almost within arm's reach, she realized that it was a skull. It was not a completely human skull. It was long and narrow with a pointy chin and narrow Asian eyes. The skull was so close to her face that it seemed she could feel its sharp edges. And in that moment, when her face almost touched the skull, she would always wake up. This particular dream tortured her. Awake, she was aware that she would dream the same dream over and over again, but the very process of dreaming always brought anxiety, blurry images, uncertainty, fear, anticipation.

She read a lot about the skulls found in Gobekli Tepe and it probably influenced her dreaming, but she couldn't understand why she often dreamed the same dream. Since it was almost dawn and she couldn't go back to sleep, she spent an hour reading. Later, she was the first one to have breakfast in a hotel restaurant.

The hotel was half empty but still people didn't hurry to go for breakfast since it was served until eleven in the morning. Mila was in a hurry. She was anxious to visit Gobekli Tepe. She ate and stayed in the hotel lobby to wait for a driver and guide who were supposed to take her to the famous archaeological site. The driver came at 7.30. The guide arrived at the same time. The guide was pleasant, talkative and obviously full of knowledge. His English was excellent.

Once they arrived to the site, he walked her around and explained to her a lot about this amazing place, considered to be the world's first temple and believed to be a burial site as well. Gobekli Tepe, at least the part that was excavated, consisted of circular and oval-shaped structure set on the hill. It was an impressive archaeological site but even more impressive were the stories, legends, mysteries, beliefs around it. Mila listened to them and didn't want to interrupt the guide even though she had hundreds of questions to ask. Finally, after a couple of hours, the guide seemed tired of walking and talking. It was getting hot. Mila knew that her tour would be over soon. She asked the guide to bring her to this site few more times and answer her questions. He agreed to meet her again the next day and bring her to Gobekli Tepe.

Mila and the guide met three more times. She would wait every morning at 7.30 in front of the hotel and the guide and driver would take her to Gobekli Tepe every of those days. The guide showed her every corner of the site. He explained everything he knew about every part of this place and answer those Mila's questions he knew the answers to. And when he didn't know what else to talk about connected to this site, he told her that he couldn't help her any further. Mila was satisfied but not completely. She thanked the guide but decided to stay in Sanliurfa few more days. She spent the next two days walking the streets of Sanliurfa, eating baklava in local restaurants, sitting in the Balikli Gol[5] park and watching and feeding the fish in the pool.

It was a late afternoon and Mila was sitting on one of the benches in the Balikli Gol park. A middle- aged woman with a child approached. The child was playing with its toys and seemed very focused on its imaginary castles with little rubber soldiers that were scattered around the ground. His mother was smiling looking at him and decided to take a rest. She came close to the bench where Mila was sitting and asked in a very good English if Mila didn't mind her sitting on the bench as well. Mila didn't mind at all and what's more she even longed for company. First, the woman seemed reserved and not willing to talk but all of a sudden, she started asking questions – where from Mila was, if she liked Sanliurfa, what brought her here, if she was married and had children. Mila politely answered all the questions but didn't talk more than what was asked by the woman. The woman seemed satisfied with the answers. Since it was hot, she opened her bag to take the bottle of water. A small picture with a strange colorful peacock fell down. Mila took it from the ground and gazed at it. It seemed familiar.

---

[5] The legendary pool of sacred fish. Known also as Abraham's Pool. According to the legends, Abraham was immolated on a funeral pyre by King Nimrod, but God turned the fire into water and the burning coals into fish. The pool of sacred fish remains to this day.

"I've seen something similar but I can't remember where..." she said.

She forced her brain to work better trying to remember where and when she saw this image or the similar one.

"It is Melek Taus[6], or the Peacock Angel," the woman said. "The Yezidis believe that Melek Taus is the true creator and ruler of the universe. The Supreme God created him as the greatest of all. Our religion is the oldest religion on earth and all other religions came after and from our religion."

Mila was more than interested to hear more about Yezidis, Melek Taus and their religion.

"So, Melek Taus is not God?" asked Mila.

"No," the woman said, "he is God's most important angel, also known as Shaitan or Satan. He is a fallen angel. He rebelled against God and was cast into Hell. But God forgave him."

"And how is Melek Taus related to Adam and Eve?" Mila was curious.

"He taught Adam and Eve secrets of worship and human evolution. He is the one who asked Adam to "eat of the grain"[7] and that's how we got wheat today."

"That's interesting," said Mila, "so you don't believe that he brought an apple, the symbol of knowledge, but wheat?" she was surprised even shocked.

"Yes, he brought the wheat that was domesticated by humans. And they stopped hunting and gathering and took up farming."

---

[6] The most important deity of the Yezidis. The Yezidis believe that they possess the oldest religion on earth, the primeval faith that features Melek Taus, and that all other religions are related to them through the Peacock Angel. The Yezidis also believe that Melek Taus is the true creator and ruler of the universe and therefore a part of all religious traditions.

[7] The passage from the Yezids Black Book also known as Mashafa Res. It is one of two books written in the style of a holy book. The other one is the Yezidi Book of Revelation.

Mila was amazed.

"And very close to Sanilurfa, in Gobekli Tepe, it all began. Gobekli Tepe was the Garden of Eden."

Mila didn't hide her bewilderment.

"Gobekli Tepe is the oldest place on earth," continued the woman persuasively.

Mila was still digesting everything she had heard from the woman for the last twenty minutes, when the woman stood up abruptly, said "nice to meet you", took the child's hand and walked away.

Mila finally stood up as well. She hurried up through the Balikli Gol park and through the busy Sanliurfa's streets and reached her hotel room. She took her laptop and the next 5 hours she spent Googling and reading the articles about Yezidis and Melek Taus and their connection to Gobekli Tepe. She learned about the Book of Enoch[8] and its story of fallen angels or Watchers[9]. And furthermore, she read about Yezidis and the commitment to their own community. She learned that they must marry within the Yezidi community, and a Yezidi who married a non-Yezidi risked the expulsion from the community. She was taking all the information and all of a sudden she remembered!

When she was a little girl, she saw a small picture of the Peacock Angel in her grandma's drawer. She also remembered

---

[8] The Book of Enoch is one of the most important non-canonical apocryphal works, and probably had a huge influence on early Christian, particularly Gnostic beliefs. Filled with hallucinatory visions of heaven and hell, angels and devils, Enoch introduced concepts such as fallen angels, the appearance of Messiah, Resurrection, a Final Judgment, and a Heavenly Kingdom on Earth.

[9] In the Book of Enoch, the Watchers are angels dispatched to Earth to watch over the humans. They soon begin to lust for human women led by their leader Samyaza. The offspring of these unions are the Nephilim, savage giants who pillage the earth and endanger humanity.

that her grandma was not in the house at that moment so she asked her grandpa what it was. After seeing the picture in Mila's hand, grandpa got furious. He grabbed the picture and asked Mila where she had found it. Mila told him the truth. Half an hour later, when grandma came back from the shop, the moment she entered the house, grandpa faced her yelling and showing the Peacock Angel picture. Mila had never seen him so angry. Grandma looked ashamed for some reason and asked Mila to go and play outside. Even fifty meters from the house, Mila could hear grandpa's angry voice. However, she saw her friend and they went to the park to play.

This memory struck her. Why did her grandma have the Peacock Angel picture? She needed some answers. She grabbed her mobile phone and called her mother. It had been a long time since she talked to her mother. Her mother knew Mila was going for some trip to Asia, but Mila had never told her where exactly she would go. Anyway, her mother answered the phone immediately. After the usual small talk, Mila asked her:

"Mum, why did grandma have the Peacock Angel picture? I remember finding it in her drawer when I was little. Do you know anything about it?"

A moment of silence.

"Mum? Was grandma a Yezidi?"

"I don't want to talk about it on the phone," said Mila's mother indifferently.

"Please I need to know," begged Mila.

"Not on the phone, Mila! We'll talk when you come back. Stay safe and call me when you're back."

She hang up. Mila was confused. She didn't fail to notice irritation in her mother's voice and a certain kind of shame.

Mila sat on the bed with the phone in her hand more than ten more minutes thinking about her conversation with her mother. When she got herself together, she turned on her laptop and booked the flight back. She needed to go back home and find out the truth. And the first flight was the next day.

The next day, she woke up soaked in sweat. The same skull dream tortured her again. It was only 7 in the morning and the driver was supposed to pick her up at 9 am and take her to the airport. She had enough time to eat delicious baklava and say good bye to Sanliurfa. The flight was long but pleasant. She read books and magazines she bought in Sanliurfa and time flied. She arrived home the next day in the evening. She couldn't wait any longer to talk to her mother and hear the whole story, so she decided to call her immediately. Luckily, her mother sounded calm and told Mila that she was welcome to come to her house and talk. Mila didn't want to lose time. She quickly took shower, grabbed one beautiful sarong she bought for her mother in Sanliurfa and called a taxi. Ten minutes later, her mother opened the door, hugged her, seated her on a couch in the living room and brought her a cup of tea. Then, she sat as well in a wing chair across from Mila. Her mother closed her eyes for a moment, then, she took a deep breath and began:

"I don't know if you remember but your grandfather was a vagabond. Always ready to travel, to move, to go somewhere. When I was a kid, he would, every second-third day, put me in his old car and take me to different places, sometimes not that far from our hometown but the other days, we would go miles and miles far from it. We visited all the lakes, rivers, cities, villages in our region and few other regions until I reached the age of nine years. When he was young he was worse. He would grab his back pack and travel the most remote places on earth. When he was 21, he went to the south-east Turkey. In that time, probably he was one of the rare Westerners to set his foot on the soil of that part of Turkey. Initially, he planned to spend just a couple of days there and to continue his trip to probably Iraq and Iran. But he got very sick. He couldn't eat, drink or move from bed. He was so weak and in pain that he was afraid he would die there. Luckily, he met a nice young man, Misha, almost his own age, who was Yezidi and this young man took him to his home where he lived with his parents and sister. First, the family was angry that their son brought a Westerner to their house who would "spoil the sacredness of their home with his Western impurity" but then they agreed to take care of him until he got better. Misha's sister was the one who was bringing food and water to your grandpa in a small room where the family put him. Even though, they couldn't communicate verbally since the young girl didn't speak English, your grandpa fell in love with her.

Anyway, the only one in the family who spoke English was Misha. Since your grandpa spent almost one month in their house lying in bed and hoping to recover, he and Misha talked a lot every day. Misha told him a lot about Yezidis, their beliefs and tradition. He told him about their commitment to the Yezidi community and ostracism of those who decided to marry a non-Yezidi. Your grandpa learned that his feelings for Misha's sister couldn't be revealed otherwise, both she and he would be in trouble. Days were passing and he wondered if the girl felt the same for him. He took a piece of paper and drew a man who was holding a flower in his hand. The next time the girl came to his room he gave her the drawing. First, after seeing the drawing, the girl looked confused and scared, but then he recognized a trace of a smile on her beautiful face. She took the drawing, folded it and put it in her pocket. The following day, he drew a man with a bunch of flowers, and the day after, a man with a heart in his hand. While taking the last drawing, the girl finally showed a real smile. But then, as if she regretted it, she ran away from the room. The next day she didn't show up. Instead of her, Misha brought food and water.

"That what you are doing is very dangerous," said Misha calmly. Your grandpa was taken by surprise. "I mean, making a young Yezidi girl fall in love with you..." he was looking your grandpa straight into the eyes, "my sister showed me the drawings you had given her...you know that we Yezidis don't mix with the other religions, beliefs, groups. If we did, the worst curse would fall on us."

Your grandpa didn't say a word. But he also couldn't help himself from falling in love with the girl. The girl didn't show up the following day either. Your grandpa was feeling better and better and he knew he would have to leave soon. He decided to risk and talk to Misha about his plan. Misha was the only one who could help him. He told Misha about his feelings for his sister and he told him that he was planning to talk to Misha's parents anyway and he needed Misha as an interpreter. Misha got angry.

"You are absolutely crazy! You really are! We are Yezidis! My parents would never let their daughter marry a Westerner! And it is not only them. But the whole Yezidi community will stand against you. And my sister will be excluded from our community and will not be allowed ever again to even come and visit any of us here."

Your grandpa was deeply disappointed and hurt. He was feeling much better physically though and he decided to leave in three days. Every next time Misha came to his room, he was quiet and seemed deep in thought.

In the evening before your grandpa's departure, Misha came to his room.

"Two days ago I spoke with my sister," he said. "She seems really likes you and is willing to run away with you."

The words "run away" struck your grandpa. He didn't plan to run away from anyone and with anyone.

"I decided to help you," Misha continued, "I made my sister a passport. Don't ask how! And she will be ready to leave with you before dawn. You have to leave before anyone is awake. So tell me, do you still want her to come with you?"

Your grandpa didn't hide surprise. He was shocked by the Misha's plan but he couldn't back out of the whole situation and honestly he didn't want to. He was young, in love, and ready for big risks.

He didn't let himself dwell on the whole idea of escape. Instead, he took the girl's passport, thanked Misha and checked if all his belongings were packed. He couldn't sleep that night at all. At 4 am, he took his backpack, jacket and hat, met the girl in the corridor and they left the house without making any noise and without waking up anyone. They walked until the end of city where they found a taxi which took them to the train station. Luckily, when they arrived, they had to wait only twenty minutes for the train to Istanbul. And even though people were staring at the Westerner and Turkish girl, everything went well. However, once they arrived here I believe you can imagine the shock of your great grandparents when their son brought a Yezidi girl to their house. But he was their only child whom they loved and supported in everything so they accepted her as his wife-to- be. But they were afraid that any moment someone might come to look for the girl and kill all of them in the house. Your great grandfather even bought special locks for the front door and a German Shepherd that stayed in the garden all night and day long. However, law was on their side since both their son and the girl were mature. Both of them were 21 years old.

After a year when they realized that no one was looking for the girl, they relaxed. Your grandpa and the girl, your grandma, got married and first they got me and a year after they got your uncle Misha. Your grandma was a very smart woman. She learned English fast and even though I remember her strange accent when I was very little, by the time you were born, her accent was perfect. No one was able to say that she had been born in Turkey. However, you have to understand and I am sure you do that her life was not easy, before or after leaving Turkey. Giving up the whole her family and Yezidi identity was heartbreaking even though it was her choice. She suffered a lot. I remember finding her crying in her bedroom while holding the picture of the Peacock Angel and asking for forgiveness. She never heard anything about her parents and brother. Once when I was ten, your grandpa suggested going to her hometown alone and finding her parents and brother and trying to talk to them and beg them to accept him as their son-in-law, and to accept their marriage. She forbade him to ever again mention something similar. She knew how dangerous it would be to go back there and useless as well. She knew that kind of attempt would have no desired effects and it would be more than disappointing. She accepted that she would never again see anyone from her family. And she lived with it. The only reminder of that old life was the picture of the Peacock Angel."

The mother stopped talking. She went to the bedroom and after a minute came back. She came to Mila and opened her hand asking her to take what was in her palm. It was a small picture of the Peacock Angel.

"When I was little I found that picture in the grandma's drawer...she and grandpa fought over it. Grandpa was very angry that she kept this picture," Mila said.

"No," the mother said, "they didn't fight over the picture. When your grandpa suggested going to find your grandma's family because he couldn't bear her suffering so much, she not only refused but asked him not to mention them again or anything that connected her to Yezidis. Years later, when you found this picture, he realized that she had never stopped suffering and probably felt guilty because she abandoned them. He was angry because she refused his help. He wanted her to stop feeling guilty and to stop suffering."

Her mother finished the story. Mila sat quietly holding the picture of the Peacock Angel. It must have been so hard for grandma to live the life with guilt and ignorance. But she didn't have other options. At least, it seemed so. The great thing was she had had a wonderful husband who loved her, children and grandchildren. She had the family that supported her, loved her, and made her life easier than the one she had led when she had been young. Some decisions were not easy to make but Mila guessed when you were young everything seemed easy. The only remnant left from her old life was that picture. And it was not a religious token as Mila had initially believed. It was a painful reminder to the old life. Her grandma kept this picture maybe to remind herself that we all did good and bad things in life. And as Yezidis believed that good and evil both exist in humans, it all depended on humans which one they chose. And even if they thought at certain moment they chose good but it was perceived as bad, they would be forgiven, as God forgave Melek Taus, the fallen angel.

Mila was happy with her own interpretation of her grandma's decisions, life, beliefs. After finishing the cup of tea, Mila kissed her mother goodbye and went home.

That night she lied in her bed eyes wide open thinking about the story her mother had told her a couple of hours ago. For a long time, she couldn't fall asleep. But once she did, she slept deeply and peacefully like a newborn baby after finishing a full bottle of milk. There was no skull dream and the morning sun rays woke her up. She got up, came to the window, opened it and let the sun sneak inside her room. She made herself a cup of black Turkish coffee, took the Black Book, sat in a wind chair next to the window, face toward the sun and started reading it:

"Wherefore, it is true that My knowledge compasses the very Truth of all that Is,

And My wisdom is not separate from My heart..."

A Violin Maker

In a small town, Cremona, in the northern Italy, a boy was born. They named him Paolo. He was born deaf.

For a deaf child, there were no many prospects. There were five children in the family and only the two oldest ones were sent to school. When he was 10, Paolo was sent to the local violin maker to help him and learn the craft of violin making. No one expected anything more from him.

The old violin maker became very fond of Paolo. He liked the boy's inquisitive mind, hard work and persistence. Even when the dark surrounded the city and the candle light was not enough to continue working, the boy would not stop. Paolo also rarely talked. There were days when the two of them didn't exchange a word or sign. And the teacher loved it. He had his own peace which was not disturbed by the boy's presence. And what was even more important, Paolo showed a great talent for violin making. As the months were passing by, the teacher noticed that his student's violins were getting better and better and he knew that one day, Paolo would be better violin maker than him. He had that rare talent for details and as if he hadn't been deaf, he could feel the wood and strings as if he had been the one to play the instrument. He would carve scrolls[10] in the most unusual ways. Rarely would he make them curly. He preferred carving leaves and flowers instead on the top of violin. And an f-hole[11] was something he did even better. This small hole that he was making helped the sound go through it so smoothly and beautifully that it seemed as if it had been a nightingale's voice. The way he was choosing the maple wood was extraordinary. He would stroke gently the piece of maple wood, and hold it in his hands for a while as if checking its pulse to see if the piece was alive enough to produce the magnificent sound. Then, he would place it on the working table, explore every corner of it, as if looking for an unacceptable deformity, and finally when he made sure there was no such a deformity, he would boil it. And he would always boil it a little bit longer and at a lower temperature than his teacher. At the beginning, his teacher was angry because Paolo didn't follow his instructions but then he let him do it his own way. After boiling the wood, Paolo did what his teacher showed him. He would use potassium silicate as a ground and then he would cover it completely with vernice bianca[12] This strengthened the inside and outside of a violin and the beloved tones later came out of it. It was a pleasure to watch him work. His hands were sliding over the wooden surface and his eyes were fixed on one specific spot, undisturbed by the noise outside. He seemed a kind of transfixed by the beauty of an artifact that he produced. He was in love with the craft of violin making. And his teacher's heart was full.

[10] A scroll is the decoratively carved the beginning of neck of certain stringed instruments, mainly members of the violin family.

[11] An F-hole is a sound hole in instruments from the violin family. It is an opening in the upper sound board.

[12] Vernice bianca is a type of sealer varnish used in violin making. It is mainly prepared with a mix of egg white and gum Arabic.

When Paolo was 18, his teacher, who was already old, got a bad fever which knocked him down.

He didn't suffer for a long time. After a few days of fighting the illness, he passed away.

After his teacher died, Paolo had to deal with so many things. All the remaining work, negotiations with customers, payments, wood supply. And he was not as good in these tasks as he was in violin making. Violin making was the only thing he knew to do very well. The teacher's cousin, Giovani, a sturdy young man, with a very red face and a lot of pimples on it, took over all the financial things and customers. But he knew nothing about violin making. The teacher used to carefully chose his clients, avoiding those new rich who had nothing to do with music but wanted to have all musical instruments displayed in their houses in order to show off. They usually had some very strange requests. They wanted the violin to be bigger or smaller than it was normal, and decorated in a ridiculous way, and made from the tree that was growing in their own garden. The teacher would just ridicule this kind of people and he would not care about how rich or powerful they were. Violin making was an artistic craft and those people didn't know anything about art. However, the teacher's cousin was greedy and sleazy and he knew that those people don't hesitate to spend a lot of money for things they wanted. And he wanted money more than anything. Paolo was not in a situation to quit what he was doing. First of all, he loved his job, and as long as he didn't have to deal with people's demands but just focus on the very process of violin making, he felt fine. And second, his family couldn't help him. They didn't have enough money sometimes, not enough even for food. He often brought them food and whatever they needed. Therefore, he decided to continue doing what he only knew to do.

In the middle of summer, when the sun was mercilessly burning the ground and heating the air, a famous rich man from Rome came to Cremona. He had heard about the deaf man who was making some of the best violins. He wanted to order one violin for his younger sister. The two of them, a brother and sister, arrived in Cremona one sunny day. They rented a house in the center of Cremona and planned to stay there for a few months, as long as it took a violin to be ready. The young man was a bit snobbish and uptight. But his younger sister, who was 16, was a lovely creature. She was not only physically beautiful, but very well-mannered, always smiling, and wishing "good day" to everyone whom she saw on the street. She was curious and loved talking with Cremona's flower sellers and people at the local market. In a few days, she got fans from all over Cremona. Everyone talked about a lovely young "signorina" Rosanna. When the brother and sister came for the first time to the Paolo's workshop, Giovani, anticipating a lot of money coming, made the workshop sightseeing tour and special speech for them. They didn't seem impressed or in-terested in hearing so much about the place, which was pretty simple and dirty, or about his cousin, Paolo's teacher, who was famous all around Italy. They were more eager to meet Paolo and order a violin for Rosanna.

They ignored Giovani and went directly to Paolo who looked at them calmly and waited to hear what they wanted. But Paolo didn't fail to notice how beautiful Rosanna was. And how kind and polite. She was smiling all the time, looking Paolo directly in the eyes, and letting her brother talk.

Paolo blushed and pretended to look at what the brother was drawing on a shabby piece of paper. But actually, he was stealthily looking over his shoulder and trying to see what Rosanna was doing.

Rosanna was looking around and touching some of violins that Paolo worked on. She was investigated them, and admired them with a smile and eyes wide open. And Paolo, seeing her excitement, knew that she was one of his kind. She loved violins and probably, she loved music. He was almost sure that she would be, if she already wasn't, a great violin player. When the brother drew everything he wanted and had to show Paolo, the two of them wished him good bye and left. Paolo's heart was beating fast. For the first time in his life, a woman, instead of a violin, impressed him and made a turmoil of his emotions.

The next few weeks, Paolo was focused on making a violin for Rosanna. He felt light-headed and was sweating every time she came to see the violin progress. She would spend an hour, sometimes two, watching Paolo working. And in her eyes, one could see that she admired his work. He wanted even to help him but he refused that. Her presence was distraction and he couldn't really stay focused on what he was doing but he loved to have her around, no matter that he was only productive when she was not there. But she was his muse and inspiration. Thinking about her, he made the perfect shape and arching of the violin. He knew that this violin would be his masterpiece. Rosanna was happy to come by almost every day and watch Paolo working. She liked the way this young man created violins. He seemed kind of talking to them in some alien and silent language that only he understood. He treated violins as if they had been alive and he touched the wood as if he had petted a dog. His movements were slow and steady. And he always seemed so focused no matter what happened around him. In some strange way, she grew very fond of him. And he let her spend time in his workshop and even communicated with her, once in a while, in his own sign language. They shared a love for violins. If he was from her own world, she would easily fall in love with him, but she avoided thinking about this because she knew that there was a world of difference between them.

The violin making took a bit longer than expected, since Paolo, on purpose, didn't hurry to finish this special violin. And Rosanna didn't complain, since she enjoyed Cremona and all its peculiarities. And she enjoyed spending time with Paolo in his workshop and watching him working. However, Rosanna's brother started getting anxious to go back to Rome. He missed parties, heavy drinking, social life that Cremona didn't offer him. He started pushing Paolo to finish the violin as soon as possible. And Paolo had no choice.

The masterpiece was ready, and both Rosanna and her brother were happy. They praised Paolo and the violin and were very generous when paying for it. Paolo didn't care about money but Giovani certainly did. Paolo was sad since he knew he might never again see Rosanna. Before they left, Rosanna came to the Paolo's workshop to say good bye. She wanted to hug him but found it inappropriate. Instead, they shook hands good bye and she gave him her white handkerchief with a small red rose flower in one corner of it. Paolo's hands were trembling and he felt as if the ground beneath him will open and swallow him. His heart was pounding fiercely in his chest. He didn't want her to go. But he had to let her go.

The next few weeks he couldn't make himself eat anything. He got sick and had to stay in bed for some days. Giovani was not happy. The clients were waiting for their violins and he wanted their money. So as soon as Paolo started feeling better, he started working again. And work helped him not to think too much about Rosanna. Or at least he thought so.

Years passed. Paolo was already in his thirties but he never met a woman that triggered his heart like Rosanna had done. He didn't think about getting married. Anyway, there were no many women who wanted a deaf husband. And he suppressed his physical desires somehow. Only he knew how he managed to do that.

One day, very early in the morning, Giovani opened the door of the workshop and entered the room where Paolo was working. He was all excited. Some strange happiness and excitement radiated from him, and Paolo knew that money must have been the reason for that. He told Paolo that "signora" Rosanna was coming to make another order. She wanted another violin. Paolo was taken completely by surprise when he heard the news. It had been so long... His heart started pounding fiercely. He touched his chest, there were he kept the handkerchief that Rosanna had given to him, in a small pocket. It was his greatest treasure. He started remembering her face, lips, eyes, cheeks, eyebrows, hair. He could see them clearly as if she had been standing in front of him. He didn't forget any part of her. He had a vivid picture of her in his mind.

The day when she arrived was one of the most exciting days in his life. A river of emotions flooded over him. However, she didn't come alone. She visited his workshop the very same day when she arrived. She came with her husband and a little girl. Like mother, like daughter. Paolo was looking at the little girl and remembered the first time Rosanna had come to his workshop. She was a bit older than her daughter now, but she had the same elegance, curiosity, smile as her mother. Paolo was happy and sad. He realized, even though, he had somehow suspected before, that she was married and not anymore that young girl who had taken his heart. But she was still gorgeous and he couldn't help noticing that he was still deep in love with her. But his heart started aching. He didn't want to see her with another man and he wanted to always keep an image of her as a young free girl.

Rosanna was very excited and honestly happy to see Paolo. She introduced him to her husband and daughter and called him a "genius". Her broad smile and shiny eyes showed Paolo that she was happy. And he felt sad that he didn't make her happy instead of someone else. But soon enough, he discarded these thoughts and told himself to stop behaving silly. He always knew that what he felt for her would never be enough. They were as different as chalk and cheese. Anyway, Rosanna wanted Paolo to make a violin for her daughter. She didn't want to draw anything or write anything. She didn't give him any instructions. She let him make the violin however he wished. He was satisfied. She trusted him.

He worked hard and didn't want to waste time. He wanted to finish his work as soon as possible. It was not that he really wanted her to leave Cremona, but her staying there also made him suffer. She had a family and her own life and he was stuck in a moment. He still loved her the way he had so many years ago. However, she would come every day to his workshop to see the progress of the violin. Sometimes she would come alone but often with her husband and daughter. One rainy day, she came to the workshop alone. Paolo tried to ignore her and didn't move his eyes from the violin he was working on. But he was not focused. His hands trembled and he couldn't calm his pounding heart. She came close to him and sat in a chair just a meter far from Paolo. He couldn't work like that and he stopped, went outside for a moment, took a deep breath and when he came back he saw her sitting in the same chair with the half-finished violin in her hands. She told him the violin already looked amazing. He didn't react to this remark. Then she left the violin where she had found it and took his hand. She told him she was sorry if she did something wrong. She told him she admired him and if the circumstance were not as they were she would fall in love with him. He didn't want to hear this. For him, she was an angel, with pure heart and pure thoughts, who didn't care about material and social differences between people. He knew that they couldn't be together, and they never could. He knew that she knew this but he didn't want to hear her telling him that. He still wanted to have the illusion of not being sure what she thought. He wanted to believe that she had got married and never showed him that she had cared about him because of the pressure form her family. He wanted to believe that they had pushed her to get married to another man. But now he knew that it had been her will. Some strange anger overcame him. He opened the door and showed her that he wanted her to leave. He couldn't work while she was there. She didn't say anything. She just left.

Paolo finished the violin in record time. He told Giovani that he would like to stay at home for few days since he didn't feel well and therefore, Giovani was supposed to deliver the violin to Rosanna and her family. Paolo didn't want to see her.

Rosanna was sad when she realized that she would not see Paolo to thank him personally. He made an absolutely beautiful violin for her daughter. But she had to accept his wish. She had no right to request more than that from him. When the day of their departure arrived, she came one more time to the workshop, which was empty and somehow sad without Paolo. She sat in a chair and breathed the air filled with the scent of maple wood. She touched the wooden pieces scattered around and finally, after half an hour, she left.

Within the next few decades Cremona got few more violin making factories. But Paolo was known as the best violin maker even though he was getting old and he couldn't keep up the same pace of work he had had when he had been younger. But clients didn't complain. They respected him and knew that his violins were worth waiting for. Paolo's health, however, started to decline dramatically.

Rosanna was a well-known violin player and violin teacher in Rome. Her daughter was a famous violin player as well and she traveled all around Europe until she finally settled down in Paris. Rosanna's husband died unexpectedly of a heart attack. Rosanna lived alone for many years. Her only companions were violins and her students. She was pretty happy but there was something that bothered her deeply. She often thought about Paolo and wondered if he ever forgave her. That thought disturbed her. And she decided to travel to Cremona and visit him.

Rosanna arrived in Cremona one beautiful April day. Cherry blossoms colored this charming city and she, for a moment, felt like a 16-year-old girl who used to talk and laugh with locals, play her violin for her brother and watch Paolo making violins. The same day she settled down in a hotel in the very center of Cremona, she decided to visit Paolo's workshop. When she came in front of it, she noticed that the outside building didn't change much since the last time she had been there. But she noticed that the workshop was closed. She walked around the building and didn't find anyone.

Since she didn't know where Paolo lived, and even if she knew she was a bit shy to go directly to his house, she decided to visit Giovni and find out why the workshop was closed. When she arrived to his house, first, he couldn't recognize her but when she mentioned her own name he remembered and apologized. Many many years passed since he had seen her. He and his wife invited her for a cup of tea. Rosanna told him that she had been to the workshop and that she was surprised to find it closed. And the man told her that it was hard for him to find an appropriate violin maker after

Paolo's death. When she heard that Paolo had died, Rosanna for a moment stopped breathing. The shock left her out of breath. Her hands started trembling and the cup she was holding fell down and broke into pieces. Giovani and his wife approached her asking if she was alright and if they should call the doctor. They laid her down on a sofa and after few minutes Rosanna started feeling better. They were surprised and a bit scared. Once she managed to sit up again, she found out that two years ago, Paolo had died of pneumonia. He had been in bed for almost a month before he had passed away. Rosanna didn't speak a lot after. She was mostly listening absent-mindedly her hosts and when she felt ready to walk again, she thanked them for hospitality and asked them to come and visit her violin music academy. She left them her card.

Giovani and his wife walked their guest to the door, and once they returned to the living room, Giovani looked at the card. The card was white with golden edges and in one corner of it, the rose was engraved. The golden letters said: "Paolo Maestri Violin Music Academy."

The Baby

My name is Wayan[13]. It means I was the first child of my parents. I was born in a small village near Batukaru Temple[14].

My family was poor so I couldn't finish high school. I had to work and help parents feed hungry children. We were 6 children. I started working as a pecalang[15]. It was not a difficult job. You just had to appear before and during some bigger ceremonies in the temple or my own village, Make sure everything is fine, to manage traffic, patrol the streets. Actually, it was pretty boring job.

But it was well paid. Plus, you could eat and drink as much as you want during those ceremonies.

---

[13] In general, Balinese people name their children depending on the order they are born, and the names are the same for both males and females. The firstborn child is named Wayan, Putu or Gede, the second is named Made or Kadek, the third child goes by Nyoman or Komang, and the fourth is named Ketut. If a family has more than four children, the cycle repeats itself and the next 'Wayan' may be called Wayan Balik which loosely translates to 'another Wayan'.

[14] Batukaru Temple, referred to by local Balinese people as Pura Luhur Batukaru, is one of Bali's key temples.

[15] Type of local security officers in Bali. They are usually engaged in mundane tasks such as traffic control, but during bigger events, they are assigned to help with general security.

When I was 20, I got married for a local girl. There was good relationship between the two families and she was pretty so why not?! She was a good woman and fine wife. She never complained, didn't talk much, prepared food regularly, took care of my mother and father and did absolutely everything that was expected from a Balinese woman. But we couldn't have kids. No matter how much we tried, went to many local balians[16] and she was taking jamu[17] , she just couldn't stay pregnant. I could not blame her, maybe it was not problem in her. Maybe I was the one to blame, but we didn't have money to go to the hospital and check what was wrong and who was the one to blame. So everything was fine. We lived without children and I was a bit sad that we didn't have them but didn't show her that ever.

We lived 10 years without kids. When I was 30, we were preparing the Galungan[18] ceremony in the village and Batu-karu Temple. I woke up very very early, before dawn, and went to the temple to check if everything was fine and wait for the other pecalang officers, my colleagues, who were supposed to work with me that day. I entered the temple when you still couldn't see anything around and strolled around just to waste some time, since I was the first one on-site. It was still a bit cold in the morning and I walked around fast to keep myself warm. You could hear only birds and roosters in the distance. No man was still there, or at least I thought so.

After 10 minutes of fast walking around the temple, while I was going to the main entrance to the temple to sit in front

---

[16] Balian is a traditional healer in Bali.

[17] Jamu is a traditional Indonesian herbal medicine made from turmeric, ginger, and other herbs.

[18] Galungan is a Balinese holiday celebrating the victory of dharma over adharma. It marks the time when the ancestral spirits visit the earth. The last day of celebration is Kuningan, when they return.

and wait for my colleagues, it seemed that I heard someone or something crying. What could it be? It was a kind of Leak[19]'s voice, high-pitched and squealing but still human-like. I started feeling nervous. It is not that I get easily scared but in that situation I can't say. I was feeling comfortable. I stopped and looked around. Nothing was moving, no other sounds, and No shadows in the dark. I was listening, trying even not to breathe in order not to disturb some mean creatures, ghosts or whoever was making that weird noise. And when I focused on the sound itself, I realized that it was a child's voice, actually a baby's cry. I was listening to where it was coming from and finally moved towards the direction of cry.

When I came close to the bush where the sound was coming from, I saw it – a tiny little wriggling thing that didn't stop crying. It was wrapped in a colorful sarong. I was not an expert for babies but it was not a new born baby. It must have been a few months old. I didn't know what to do. I was standing there for a couple of minutes totally flabbergasted, looking at the baby and wondering what to do. Finally, I knelt and picked up the baby. I was holding it. And it stopped crying. Not sure for how long I stayed there holding the baby, but I know that I heard voices and people gathering in front of the temple. Then, I decided to bring the baby in front of them.

My colleagues and people who knew me were surprised, or even shocked, when they saw me with a baby. The women approached the baby and me first. They started throwing hundreds of questions but I was too shocked myself to answer

---

[19] Leak or Leyak is a horrifying demon in the Balinese mythology. Steeped in black magic, a Leak can appear as an ordinary human by day, but by night, it takes a terrifying form: a disembodied, menacing head with great fangs and bulging eyes hovering in the air, with the entrails of the body still attached and floating beneath it.

any of them. When I finally pulled myself together, I told them that I found the baby inside the temple. People started debating what to do and everyone agreed that we needed the opinion and instructions of pemangku, the temple priest. We waited half an hour for the pemangku to arrive. In the meantime, some women changed holding the baby and walking around with it, and even a bottle of milk appeared from somewhere so everyone was watching women feeding the baby and singing some lullabies.

When the pemangku arrived, he was approached by few older men from our village who probably told him what had happened. The pemangku came close to me and the group of women who were busy carrying around and feeding the baby and asked me to come with him. The pemangku, some village elders and I sat down in one far corner of the temple. The pemangku and elders asked me to tell them how I had found the child and I told the whole story. Then, there was a moment of silence. Everyone seemed to be thinking. And I was thinking loudly. I mentioned that there were no women in our village who had a baby and would do this. No crazy people who would give up their child.

The pemangku and elders discussed for a while and concluded that it would be the best to check other villages as well. So, they sent other pecalangs to patrol other villages and talk with people and check if there was any household with a baby missing. The pemangku asked me if I would be so kind to bring the baby home and if my wife and I would take care of it just a day or two until the parents were found or some solution. He said that the banjar[20] would help giving us some money to buy food and clothes for the baby. I accepted. It

---

[20] Banjar is the smallest administrative unit of vast bureaucracy in Bali.

might not have been something I really wanted to do but I felt that I needed to help this little crying creature find its parents.

When I arrived home that day in the afternoon, I met my wife in the garden who seeing what or actually whom I was carrying almost stumbled on a rock and fell down. She approached the baby and me and asked to hold it while I was telling her the whole story.

"This is a sign of gods, Wayan." she said excitedly. I didn't say anything because I didn't know what to say. The next two days, my wife and I entertained ourselves feeding the baby. The baby was not crying much except when we were supposed to go to sleep. Somehow, this little girl (it was a baby girl), loved nights. So, it meant no sleep for us. But we didn't complain. Somehow, we started getting fond of that little thing and we knew that they would take it away from us sooner or later. On the third day, the pemangku came to our house and said that they still hadn't found the parents and asked if my wife and I would be so kind to take care of the baby just few more days. He planned to talk with the authorities and see what they suggested. Of course, both my wife and I said 'yes' without thinking. This baby was getting under our skin every day a bit more.

More than a week passed, and the pemangku came back. He told me that the authorities suggested putting the baby in an orphanage until someone appeared and adopted it. My heart sank. I didn't want this little baby girl to end up in some dirty orphanage where she would be maltreated and always hungry. Without even asking my wife for an opinion (and I knew she would agree), I asked the pemankgu what the chances were we kept the baby instead sending it to the orphanage.

The pemangku looked at me surprisingly and said he would have to talk about that with some other pemangkus and authorities as well. And he left.

My wife and I discussed and agreed that we both wanted to keep the baby. We didn't have our own children and this as my wife said "sign of gods" was something that brought some special warmth to our home. We were so happy to have that little girl.

After one week, the pemangku returned. He was smiling and I realized that he was bringing me good news. And I was right. Since there were no parents looking for a missing baby anywhere in Bali and orphanages were full of abandoned children, the best thing for this little girl was to stay with my wife and me.

"You are a good man, Wayan, and your family is respected in the whole area, so it was not hard for me to persuade the authorities," said the pemangku. I thanked him and promised that my wife and I would take care of the little girl as if it had been our own child. The pemangku smiled and said he knew that already. While leaving he just added something:

"You have to know that there is a chance that her parents or one of them might, one day, come to look for her, even though I doubt it will happen. But I just want you to be prepared for something like that."

I nodded and walked him to his motor bike.

The next few months, it was not an exaggeration to say that my wife and I were the happiest people not only in our village but in the whole Bali. We couldn't have our own children but gods pitied us and sent us this little girl. And we named her Dewi[21]. She was our little goddess. Dewi was growing fast and when she started walking she brought such liveliness to our household. She was running after chicken in the garden, trying to help her Ibu[22] prepare cananag sari but it was more ruining the banana leaves instead of helping her mother but

---

[21] Dewi in Indonesian means "goddess".

[22] Ibu in Indonesian means "mother" or "madam" or "lady".

she didn't mind. She would just smile and seeing Dewi destroying another banana leaf tell her: "You are still small, you will learn to make offerings one day."

And years were passing by, Dewi was growing and no one was appearing to look for her. My wife and I lived a happy life.

Our village was small and people knew one another. Every foreigner or stranger was easily noticed. When Dewi was ten, I started seeing around our village a young woman whom I didn't know and hadn't met before but there was something familiar in her face, especially in her eyes. I saw her in the local market, on the street, close to the school where Dewi was going every day. And the fear in me started growing. I was fearing that these moments would come, expecting them and avoiding them. And I was hoping and praying that they would never come. One day, while I was in my garden repairing the fence which was broken and my wife was making canang sari[23] in front of our house, the same woman appeared in front of our gate. She was just standing there not even trying to hide and staring at our garden. I left the unfinished work and approached her. I opened the gate and asked her if she was looking for someone. She remained silent and bowed her head.

"I know who you are." I said. Both of us were standing few moments without pronouncing a word.

Finally, she said: "I am sorry."

I asked her to come in and she followed me. We came to the place where my wife was making canang sari and I asked her to sit down. And then she started her story.

---

[23] Canang sari is one of the daily offerings made by Balinese Hindus to thank their gods in praise and prayer. Canang sari offerings ca be seen everywhere: in the Balinese temples, on small shrines in houses, and on the ground or as a part of a larger offering.

She was only fifteen when she met a Javanese man who was working on a construction near her house in Singaraja[24]. She fell in love with him and they started seeing each other every day after her school and when he finished work. One day, she found out that she was pregnant. She told him that and he didn't hide his shock. He admitted her that he had a wife and two children in Java but that he was willing to bring her to Java as well to become his second wife. The girl didn't expect to hear that he was married and she was deeply disappointed. But she realized that she was in trouble and that she needed to tell her parents.

When her parents heard her story, they got not only angry but her father broke a window throwing his shoes at its glass. Their only daughter fell in love with a Muslim and was carrying his child! And she herself was still a child! His anger totally took control over him and he hit his daughter. She fell on the floor and when he came to his senses and realized what he had done, ashamed he retrieved to the room in the back of house. Her mother was crying. And she followed her husband. The girl felt abandoned, lost, devastated. She didn't know what to do.

The next day, her father sent her to the village where her grandparents lived. He ordered his mother to prepare a special concoction for her and help her get rid of baby she was carrying. The girl was crying. She couldn't do that. She couldn't kill the child she carried. She decided to run away. She ran away to the south of Bali where she found a job in a small hotel as a room cleaner. She didn't tell her boss that she was pregnant and the first 6 months she was safe since her stomach was not big. But then after the 6th month she had to admit that she was pregnant. Her boss was a nice man and he told her that

---

[24] Singaraja is the largest city in North Bali.

she could stay and work easier jobs as long as she was capable of working but then when the time came for her to deliver the baby she would have to leave. And she did it. The trouble came when she felt the contractions and had to go to hospital to give the birth. She didn't have enough money for medical services but her colleagues decided to collect the money and they took her to the hospital. After delivering the baby, her troubles continued. She didn't have enough money to survive another month. She started begging for money on the street carrying the baby in her arms. And one day when she saw her own cousin from Singaraja on his motor bike something broke in her. She started crying and crying and roaming the streets with a hungry baby in her arms. She couldn't handle to live like that any longer. She decided to leave the baby in a place where she knew someone would find it soon enough so that the baby didn't die from hunger or get attacked by some animals. Before dawn, when there was still no one awake she went to Batukaru Temple and left the baby there. There was supposed to start a big ceremony in the temple just in a few hours and she knew that soon after she left someone would come and find the baby. And she was right. Just half an hour after she left the baby, Wayan found it.

The girl stopped talking. Her face was covered in tears and she couldn't stop sobbing. My wife brought her a glass of water and sat next to her holding her hand. I felt a deep sadness for this woman who was so young and whose life's hardships made her so old that she carried years of sorrow in her heart, I asked her where she lived now, with whom and if she got married again and she continued her story.

When she left the baby, she went back to Singaraja and begged her parents to take her back. She didn't mention the baby so her parents thought that she had got rid of it before it was born. They took her back and after a few months they arranged her marriage. They married her to a local man who was much older than her but was a good man. They got two children and they lived a simple life. She had never told him the story of baby. Actually, she had never told anyone. The Javanese man went back to Java a long time ago and she had never heard of him again, and he didn't know what had happened to the baby either. But the untold truth and decision to leave the child never gave her peace. She was a living ghost, never smiling, rarely talking and somehow alive only when surrounded by the other two children. She couldn't stand any longer living like that. She had to find out what had happened to her baby after she had left it. So, she started coming to Batukaru Temple more often, talking to people, walking around villages around the temple, looking at children's faces and hoping that she would find her own eyes in one of those faces. And one day, it happened. She was sitting in a local warung[25] in front of village school and drinking coffee. The children started coming through the school gate which meant that the classes were finished. Two girls came to the warung, bought some ice tea and sat on the chairs opposite her. And then, the woman recognized her! It was her child! The eyes, the lips, her forehead...everything. And she stayed there motionless staring at the girl. Long after the two girls were gone, the woman remained sitting and staring into the distance. She kept coming back whenever she could. She saw sometimes Wayan or his wife waiting for the girl after school and one day, she followed them and saw where they lived. It took her two months to pick up courage and appear in front of their gate.

---

[25] Warung is a type of small family-owned business – a small restaurant or café, in Indonesia.

The woman stopped talking and she lowered her head looking at the ground.

"What do you want now? I asked her a bit coldly.

"I don't know...I just wanted to make sure she was alive, and she had someone to take care of her. I just wanted to see her." She retorted with a weak voice.

I started fidgeting around. I couldn't stay calm.

"Well, we raised her. She is like our own child, so you can't ask us to give her back to you...she is our everything..." I blurted out.

"No, you don't understand," she said, "I couldn't ask you that even if I wanted. I can't ask you to do that. Not only because you raised her and I left her, and because you are more her parents than I am, but because no one knows about her. No one from my family...I don't think it will be easy for any of them to accept that she exists. I don't know...I don't know...I just wanted to see her..." And she started crying again.

When all of us calmed down, I told her: "Dewi is now at school, but you can come back in a few days and you can see her. We will tell her that you are a cousin."

The woman gave a faint smile, thanked me and left. My wife and I remained silent for a long time. We didn't talk and we didn't know what to talk about, or at least, how to find the solution for the current situation. We continued with our chores silently.

That evening, we finally talked and agreed to remain strong in whatever came upon us. We prayed together and that evening spent a bit more time with our Dewi afraid that we might lose her. After a few days, the woman came back. She was feeling better and there was no sign that she would start crying or lose her control in front of Dewi. When she met Dewi, she was obviously emotional but she was handling it well and even led a normal conversation with Dewi asking her about school, friends and games she liked to play. Everything went well and I was flooded with relief. While leaving the woman asked if we would allow her to come and visit us once in a while, not too often but often enough not to become stranger again. My wife and I looked at each other and told her that she was welcome to come. She was coming once or twice per month. Dewi had got used to her and considered her her favorite "cousin". Then, one day Dewi asked her why she didn't bring her children so they could play together with Dewi. My wife, the woman and I exchanged glances. We didn't know what to say first, but then, we kind of silently agreed that the woman could bring her children sometimes. The next time, she came with a girl who was 3 years younger than Dewi but looked like her so much that we were afraid that people, our neighbors, might start talking and come to the conclusion that our "cousin" was not really our cousin. Again we were worried for no reason. The girls were playing and had good time together. Once, the woman came with her son but he was too small and his games were not the games Dewi wanted to play so they didn't get to play much together, but at least, Dewi met her brother. The woman showed no intention to do anything else except visiting Dewi and us. And somehow, we grew fond of her. We really started considering her our "cousin" and actually she was that since our daughter was her blood.

Years passed and nothing changed. We continued our lives and accepted the woman's regular visits. And my wife and I often thought how lucky and grateful we were. We couldn't ask for more. And what will be once Dewi grows up? Will we tell her the truth? Well, yes, I suppose so.

She deserves to know it. And what will happen then? Well, I guess nothing. She will decide what to do. But that's future and we should think about present and this what is now. Future will take care of itself.

Waterfall Prayer

When the first time I came to Lefkada, I was only six. My parents loved this Greek island and they spent every next holiday there. Peaceful and sleepy, it breathed in hushed tunes. I went with them every next year in summer time until I was fifteen and then I decided that I was old enough that I didn't want to spend a vacation with my parents. It was embarrassing for a teenager to spend summer with his or her mum and dad.

My teenage years were a bit rebellious and wild. Belief that we were born to be wild and free overcame me. For no reason, I fought with my father. Or at least, the reasons were banal and ridiculous. His telling me that smoking was bad for my health would make me break a glass as a signal of protest and disagreement. Yes, I am ashamed of it. But I was a teenager like everyone else and some things we do as teenagers, later we are ashamed of. Those wild years took its toll though.

I finished the high school and went to the university in the capital, Athens. My family house was not that far from Athens, anyway. Around thirty kilometers from it. I could have gone home whenever I wanted but I rarely did it. My university life in the capital was full of looseness, lack of control, experiments with drugs, weird trials driven by fashion rather than personal desire, emotional outbursts, odd and eccentric behavior. I dated a man who was beating me up. And when finally, I ended up in hospital after he had used me as his "punching bag" and tried some knockdowns, I woke up from my nightmare life. At last.

After four days in hospital, I packed my things, left Athens and went back home. I can't say that my parents were surprised to see me. Actually, they were shocked by my appearance, and for good reason. I looked like a truck had run over me. And it must have been terrifying to see your child in that condition. I was a walking zombie. Pale, bruised, scarred, in stitches. My mother took a great care of me. She behaved as if I had been her little girl, her little Eleni, who had had a bad flu and needed attention of her mum. And I am forever grateful for everything she had done for me.

She made me soups that tasted heavenly. She gave me some herbal drinks that did miracles to my body, and most of all she was there for me. She talked to me, cried with me, yelled at me and after hugged me. There's no greater bond than the one between a mother and her child.

When I got fully recovered physically and was on the good way to recover mentally, I started helping my mother in the garden. We had a kind of an oasis behind the house where the greenery took over the products of human hands. No walls, concrete walkways, wires or pipes were visible in that oasis. It seemed as if plants and bushes had wanted to cover and hide everything that had not been green. More than half a year, I was my mum's helper in the oasis. Then, one day, she asked me:

"Eleni, why don't you take a break of all this gardening and go to spend some days in Lefkada? It is May and there's no one in the house we used to rent every year. And I am sure the owners would let you stay for a small amount of money. Plus, almost no tourists in Nidri in this time of year, and I am sure you will enjoy it. It is so peaceful now there."

First, I didn't want to think about it. I was happy helping my mum in our oasis. But she was right. For more than six months, I hadn't moved anywhere. I didn't go even to the center of town or to any place near our hometown. I spent months at home and I guess it was time to go outside and breathe some different air. It was time for me to be on my own just for a while. I needed to face the world that had been a bit cruel to me the year before. But I had to deal with the fact that not the entire world was a dark place or all people except my parents were evil. I had to get rid of that fear that had crept through me after being beaten up almost to death. And I decided to go.

I arrived in Nidri on beautiful sunny Sunday. Nidri was a sleepy little town, almost always uncrowded even in the busiest months of July and August. Its white pebbled beaches, orange and lemon plantations and small waterfall up in the hill were my favorite parts of Nidri. When I had been kid those had been my favorite places. I had run along those dreamy beaches, swum in the warm water, picked up oranges and lemons from the trees and devoured them like a monkey. And I had often gone to the waterfall with my parents. We had loved to wake up very early and walk to the waterfall before the sun started burning not only the ground but our bodies as well. And those days had been probably the best days of my life.

I wanted to revive those days and I promised myself that I would do everything I had done in Nidri when I had been a little girl.

The house where my parents and I had used to stay was renovated. It was painted light blue and the new modern furniture replaced the old heavy wooden pieces. I couldn't feel that lavender scent that had sneaked into the house a long time ago. That scent had used to make me drowsy and I would often take a nap on the balcony while watching the seagulls. In that state between sleeping and being awake I would drift into a half dream while the heavy summer air had cooled off. The evening hours would bring me back to the beach and I would collect pebbles which later I had brought back to the garden and spread them around making some weird pebbly figures. I had admired those figures. They had been my masterpieces.

The first thing I did that day was buying a lavender essential oil. I filled the bowl at the top of an oil burner with water. Then, I poured a couple of drops of the essential oil in it. And I let the sleep-inducing fragrance float around the house. I was not tired. I just wanted to feel that scent. In the evening that day, when the sun started setting, I went to the beach. The edge of the sun was slowly disappearing below the horizon. I started collecting pebbles, slowly moving along the beach. There were no many people at the beach. A couple of fisherman and a mother with her child.

After collecting the pebbles for more than half an hour, I sat on the jetty and watched the last pieces of orange daylight. The sky colors were magnificent. An older lady approached me and wished me good evening. Then, she sat on the jetty as well, a bit further from me, folded her legs into a meditation position and closed her eyes. I didn't want to disturb her meditation, so I slowly stood up and walked away on the beach at dusk.

The next morning, I woke up at six, had my cup of coffee and headed to the waterfall. The crisp morning air was pleasant for longer walk. I walked slowly and didn't meet anyone on the way to the waterfall. People were asleep, enjoying the last moments of their night rest which soon would be pleasantly and modestly disturbed by bird song and bright sunlight.

I arrived at the waterfall around seven. This time, probably the spring rainfall had been heavy, since the flow was abundant when compared to those that I had seen as a kid.

I was standing there in front of the fall admiring it. And then I heard someone approaching me from behind. I turned around and saw the old lady whom I had met the day before on the jetty.

"Lefkada has an abundant storage of underground water. That is the main reason why this island is so green and lush. And that is the reason for many cascading waterfalls." She smiled. "My name is Leora."

"I am Eleni. Nice to meet you." I replied. "I saw you meditating last night on the jetty."

"Yes, I remember seeing a young woman but it was a bit dark and I am not that young anymore. My vision is not that good anymore. But my mind is in tune with my body. Much more now than when I was your age." She was talking slowly and tranquilly. There was some pleasant aura of peacefulness that she spread.

"Do you often mediate?" I asked humbly.

"Yes, meditation is not only my everyday practice, it is my way of living. I chose to follow the Buddhist path many years ago and chose to practice mindfulness and meditation every day. Mindfulness gave me my life back."

I loved her calmness and saint-like figure. She had a graceful old-age beauty. Her face was thin and tight. It didn't reveal many lines of age. And her short white hair glimmered like a snow- drenched field and matched the shape of her face. Her watery blue eyes seemed so serene that only looking at them made you feel calm.

She looked around herself and said: "I love this place. I come her every morning to meditate. This is the perfect place to start your mindfulness practice."

"And you've been practicing it since you were a child?" I was curious.

"Oh, no, my dear. I've been practicing it the last thirty years. When I was your age my life was much different. It was not a good life." She lowered her gaze and looked at the ground as if the veil of shame had cast its shadow over her. "I was a different person then, and if I didn't wake up one day and find this path that I am following now, I would be probably dead."

I looked at her surprisingly. And I wanted to ask her many things but I was ashamed to do that. Instead, I asked her if I could sometimes join her in mediation, if it didn't bother her. She gleefully said: "We can start now, if you are willing." I was willing.

We found a nice sport where we sat. And Leora guided me into meditation. I knew it would be hard but I didn't know it would be that hard.

While I was listening to her voice that instructed me what to do next, I felt comfortable and at peace. I followed the soft tunes of it and my thoughts were occupied doing what she said. My eyes were closed, and I breathed deeply and slowly. But once she let me to my own, my thoughts started roaming again. They overpowered me and I couldn't take control over them. I kept trying and every time I seemed to succeed and focus again on breathing and calmness, my mind would, after a while, wander off. I felt so frustrated and disappointed with myself.

After our meditation I told her that. Leora just smiled complacently and said:

"Even if the mind wanders or is distracted, keep trying to bring it back to the point quite gently... And even if you did nothing during the whole of your meditation but keep bringing your mind back, though it went away every time you brought it back, your meditation hour would be very well employed."

During the next couple of days, I continued spending time with Leora. We would walk every morning to the waterfall and meditate. I learned a lot about Leora.

A long time ago, she was a troublesome young woman. She was a part of a hippie gang.

They uncontrollably experimented with drugs and unprotected sex. She got pregnant and irresponsible as she was in that time, wild and believer in free love, she also wanted to be free of obligations. She was not ready to be a mother. She gave a birth to a child and let it in an orphanage. Many years later, when she tried to find her, since she had given birth to a baby girl, they told her that the baby had died one week after she had left her. That was something she couldn't get over.

Even while she was telling me about it, I felt that her heart grew heavy and cold with the burden of guilt and regret. But she took a deep breath and became herself again. She said: "We can't change what we did in the past that we are not proud of. We often carry a mental reminder of our mistakes and losses everywhere we go. And we often don't realize how much that heavy mental burden steals of our contentment. We can't change the past. What happened in our past happened. We need to learn how to move forward. It has been a hard and painful journey for me." She signed. "I could have continued ruining my life. I could have drunk myself or drugged myself to death. I could have got some deadly disease. Luckily, I chose this path that I am following now. I learned the simple techniques of posture, breath and mindfulness. There were hard days and one thing is certain – mindfulness is not easy. It doesn't come naturally. That's why it requires a lot of practice. But it is a practice for the whole of life. Through mindfulness, we learn to maintain a moment-by-moment awareness of our thoughts, feelings, bodily sensations and environment. And we learn how to find a different way to respond to experience throughout our day."

Time with Leora, our talks, meditation which improved slowly day by day, were the real therapy for my soul. I felt not only better, I felt like never in my life. I became aware of everything around me and in me. I got some encouraging positivity that guided me throughout the day. And I smiled and laughed more.

Leora told me that her biggest wish was to go to China, to see the Great wall and then visit Tibet and Himalayas. She wanted to experience Tibetan culture and to see the beauty of the worlds whose heritage in history, culture, traditions and natural beauty were well known. When she talked about that I saw in her eyes the great desire that led her. That wish was something that this woman was able and probably would do. No matter of her age, she was energetic, enthusiastic and determined. Just listening to her inspired me to start living my life the way I wanted. And I made a resolution. The first thing I would do was to finish the university. I had only one year left to finish it and get a bachelor's degree.

My holiday in Lefkada had come to an end. I said goodbye to Leora and promised to come back next year, hopefully with a university diploma in my hands. Days in Lefkada were a journey of self-revelation and I enjoyed every single moment spent with Leora. I was ready and eager to go back and finish university. I was ready to do something more than ever.

Studying was easier with meditation sessions that I practiced every day. I felt happier, lighter, brighter, more positive and calmer. I led lighthearted conversations with people I met and they seemed to be enjoying my company. I even made my mum start meditating. Everything seems much easier with that self-awareness. It became easier for me to understand other people, and myself, of course. I knew what I wanted and I put efforts to obtain it. But with calmness and emotional stability. There was no that emotional turmoil that had chased me when I had been younger.

I completed my studies within a year and I was proud of myself but not conceited. I was a merry young woman.

In July, my mum and I packed our suitcases and went to Lefkada. I wanted my mother to meet Leora.

When we arrived in Nidri, we settled down, unpacked our things and went to see Leora. But we didn't find her at home. Her house was locked and her neighbors told us that she hadn't been at home the last two months. They said they were afraid she maybe had drowned in the sea or something bad had happened to her and they seemed worried. They mentioned that her sister had been there a couple of weeks ago and she had mentioned that her documents (ID card, passport, driving license were missing). The neighbors said that Leora's sister had called the police but up to now there had been no news about Leora.

I was sad that I would not see her and that my mum would not meet her. But I deeply believed that Leora went missing for good reason. A little bit of worry might have troubled me. But Leora was a special woman and her paths were the ones she decided to take. Whatever happened, I knew it had been her wish.

The next morning, my mum and I went to the waterfall. We both meditated, but this time, I also prayed that Leora was on her way to make her dreams come true. I prayed that she was on the path of her life, smiling and thinking about me.

A Wolf's Tooth

All the other shepherds returned to the villages long time ago. But it was a nice late August day and Vlado wanted to stay a bit longer on the green slopes of the Carpathian Mountains. Just before the sun started setting, he heard his dog Rorik barking angrily. It was not a regular Rorik's barking. It was getting higher and higher in pitch and Vlado knew that Rorik was getting more upset with every new barking sound. Vlado was listening carefully where his dog's voice came from and when he was on his way to the southern side of field, the barking became growling. Anger mixed with fear. And it didn't last long. After a few minutes, Rorik was helplessly yelping. Vlado's heart was beating fast. He was calling his dog almost in panic. He knew what was going on. Rorik must have been surrounded by wolves. Vlado was scared. He had seen them many times. They would appear somewhere in distance, like silhouettes, they would appear and disappear in woods and bring a commotion among the sheep.

This time, Vlado heard terrified bleating. His sheep was frightened of the wolves. Vlado prayed his sheep to stay together. He knew very well how wolves tried to split sheep from their flock. They knew that a sheep was helpless if singled out. Vlado was scared but he tried to remain calm. Rorik was still yelping and screaming as if in fear and pain but Vlado couldn't leave the flock. He stayed close to his sheep holding the stick in his right hand and looked around. Glowing eyes were flashing from the woods. He couldn't count them well but there were at least six pairs of those devilish eyes. If he had only had a rifle!

He was squeezing the wolf's tooth in his pocket and he thought about his father. That same tooth was his father's trophy. He had killed the biggest wolf in these mountains. No one had remembered seeing bigger and more ferocious creature in the Carpathian Mountains. And the tooth was the proof. It was long and sharp like those that, once upon a time, saber-toothed tigers had had.

People in the village said that that wolf had been hunted and chased for many years by many good hunters and it always had managed to trick them and run away. But Vlado's father had got it. And he had become a local legend in the Carpathian Mountains. His father had died but he had left this tooth to his youngest son, Vlado. And Vlado carried it everywhere and kept it close as if it had been some kind of lucky charm that protected him and encouraged him.

Even this time, when fear crept through his body and paralyzed his legs, he squeezed the tooth and whispered: "I'm not afraid of you."

He dug deep into his pocket and took matches. He had to make a torch. He grabbed one of the greener sticks he had, and coated the end of the stick with the bark from the tree nearby under which he had been resting earlier. Then, he took off his T-shirt, tore it off, and one piece of it started wrapping around the end of the stick until it created a bulge in the cloth and tucked in the end of the cloth. It took him few minutes to light his torch since his torn-off T-shirt was a bit sweaty. It was hot outside and he had worn it the whole day. When finally, he managed to light the torch, he started running towards the woods where he had seen those scary eyes. And he saw them again. They were kind of moving but they didn't seem scared by him and his torch. The villagers talked that there were those wolves which were not scared of men. They were demons. The villagers believed that they could devour within minutes a grown-up man.

Vlado was slowly approaching the woods holding the torch high over his head. He knew he was not supposed to leave his flock alone. He had to stay close to it and protect his sheep. He was waving the torch around hoping to make the wolves back up. But they were not backing up further. On the contrary, one of the wolves, with the hunger in his eyes and sharp canines protruding out over his lower lip, approached slowly the flock. The sheep started moving backwards. They were petrified. The sight of an approaching predator made their blood run cold. And while the other sheep were moving in the opposite direction from the wolf, one of them remained motionless. It seemed as if the wolf's glowing eyes had paralyzed it. Vlado started yelling and running towards the wolf. He yelled so loudly that the whole mountain echoed. He grabbed a rock and threw it with all the strength he could gather directly at the wolf. But it was late. The wolf attacked the sheep and grabbed its rear leg. The poor sheep was whirling and bleating desperately. For a moment Vlado felt hopeless and tears started filling his eyes. He squeezed the wolf's tooth so tightly that it almost cut his palm.

And then, all of a sudden, Vlado heard the sound of rifle fire. The wolf fell back down. But then it stood up again and leaped towards the woods. The bullet probably just wounded the wolf. But it was not a deadly wound.

Vlado turned around and saw his brothers running towards him. His oldest brother, Stevo, carried the rifle. He asked

Vlado if he was all right and when Vlado nodded, they hurried towards the wounded sheep. The middle brother, Anton, was already there and he was holding the sheep. "It will survive, but not sure what will be with its leg. It is totally destroyed." The blood was dripping down the sheep's leg leaving the red spots on Stevo's blue T-shirt and khaki pants. "Maybe we can save it. I will take care of it when we get home."

Vlado looked at his brothers and the tears of relief ran down his cheeks. He was ashamed of crying in front of them, but they understood how it felt to be surrounded by those ferocious animals. Stevo patted Vlado's back and tried to calm him down. "You did well. You managed to save all the sheep. And I am telling you, there were more than six wolves out there. They could have devoured not only the sheep but you as well." But Vlado was afraid that he couldn't save Rorik. He headed toward the place where previously he had heard Rorik sad yelping. When he came close to the place, he saw the bloody traces on the ground and just few meters further, Rorik was laying helplessly. He knelt and touched his dog. Rorik's body was still warm, but his heart was not beating. Vlado couldn't save him. His heart ached. Rorik had died in pain. But he had tried to protect Vlado and the sheep. Vlado breathed in deeply and then breathed out a sorrowful puff of air. Only then, Vlado realized that he was still squeezing tightly the wolf's tooth. He released the grip and took it out of his pocket. He was grateful to have it. But he was more grateful to have his brothers.

TROUBLED WORLD

A Runaway

It all started when I was 7. As far as I remember, my parents were fighting and arguing all the time. They couldn't talk normally, actually, I think they couldn't stand each other. I wonder how and why they stayed together and why in the first place they had got married. Well, maybe the first few years before I was born, things had been different between them. By the way, they named me Igor, but that is not so important for this story.

Just a day after my 7ᵗʰ birthday, there was a big fight between them. They were yelling, breaking cups, plates, bowls, throwing at each other chairs and storming that it seemed the whole house was shaking. I had enough and decided to run away from that house. I packed, in my small school backpack, some things I couldn't leave behind. For a seven-year-old kid, the treasures are his favorite toy, book, half-eaten chocolate, basketball cap of his favorite team, a pair of socks and a rain coat. Luckily, it was spring so I didn't have to worry about cold weather. I didn't have any plan where to go and I just went out and started walking along the main road. It was the late afternoon and after 15 minutes of walk, I realized that it would get dark soon. But I kept walking. On the way, I met some of the people from our hometown and politely wished them good afternoon and it seemed no one noticed that I was running away. I even met my friend and his mum. They were probably on the way to the hospital since that day at school he was not feeling well and the teacher called his mum. When I met them his eyes were red and his nose was running and he was carrying a handkerchief. After 30 minutes of walking, I left my hometown. I passed by the shoes factory and petrol station and continued walking towards villages that we often passed when we went to visit our cousins in the big city which was just half an hour by car far from our hometown. But on foot, it would probably take much much longer. I remember that I was already maybe even half a way to the big city when it started getting dark. It must have been dangerous walking along the road with not many street lights since cars were stopping and people were asking me if I got lost or need a ride, but I told them that I was fine and that my house was in the first village from there and my parents didn't let me enter a car of people I didn't know. So they would just leave me alone and continue driving. I must have been walking for more than 2 hours and I was getting tired and thirsty.

I realized that, stupid me, I didn't bring any water. But luckily, I had some pocket money. I saw a small shop not that far from the main road, at the entrance to some village. I turned away from the main road and I went to the shop to buy some water. The girl who worked there seemed surprised since she probably knew everyone in the village and she didn't know me. She asked me where I was going and I told her I was going to visit my grandma in the village next to this one. She seemed like not believing my story but she didn't say anything. I bought the bottle of water and continued walking. Finally, I started feeling tiredness kicking me. I was looking around and couldn't see any place where I could sleep. There were just big houses in distance and nothing else next to the road, so

I continued walking. Another half an hour of walking and I couldn't stand it any longer. Finally, I saw some shack next to the main road. It was a bit spooky and all in ruins but I just needed a place to hide and roof over my head in case it started raining. I opened the door and put my rain coat on the ground next to the open door. I decided to sleep next to the open door just in case. I fell asleep immediately and I woke up very early in the morning when the sun started creeping through the open door. I ate the rest of the chocolate I had and continued walking along the road. But not for long. After five minutes of walking, a car stopped next to me and I saw my parents and a police officer in it. What can I say?! My running away was unsuccessful and when we got home, my father slapped me few times pretty hard but instead of me, my mother was crying until evening.

My next running away from home happened when I was 12. My father taught me to ride a motor bike. He had some old motor bike that he used to ride around the town and after begging him every day, he finally accepted to teach me how to ride it. It was pretty easy and after few days I got so confident that I drove it too fast. I know it was stupid but I was only 12. My mum was not happy that the father let me drive it alone and they fought over it. At the end of summer, my father came home very late and he was very drunk. I was in my room getting ready to sleep when I heard him and mother yelling. Then, someone hit someone else and shouting became even worse. Again, there were broken glasses, slammed door and a lot of yelling. I couldn't stand it. I sneaked out of my bed, put on my jeans, T-shirt and jacket, took my backpack and packed few chocolate bars and a bottle of water, another T-shirt, my reading glasses, the book I was reading and I went to the garage. I pulled out my dad's motor bike and waited when the shouting was loud enough to start it. I was almost sure both my mother and father didn't hear me starting the engine since their yelling prevailed over other sounds. I started driving toward the center of our town. I didn't have any specific plan where to go. I just wanted to ride. It made me feel so free. It distracted me from thinking about anything. I felt as if my brain had been empty, no thoughts, no thinking, no pressure, no headache. Just wind in my face. But I guess I was not focused on the road. And the last thing I remember from that drive was the tree in front of me. After that I woke up in hospital. They told me I was lucky since I did hit the tree but I was not driving fast so I ended up only with a broken arm. It was not very successful attempt to run away.

When I was 17, I finally finished high school and I decided to go to the university in the furthest city north from my hometown. That was not the most beautiful city and the university was not the best one but I needed to go somewhere far far far away from everything that I had known and that had surrounded me the last 17 years. I got the scholarship and moved there. During the first year of my studies I came to my hometown once in few months, but then those visits became less frequent. My parents didn't push me to visit them either, so everything was fine for all of us. After I had finished my studies, I found a decent job in the same city and stayed there. One rainy day, after work, my mother called me. She told me that the father had passed away. He had been drinking too much the last few years. Luckily, I was not there to witness his alcohol-fueled outbursts. But poor mum. She was the victim of his craziness and violence. I felt guilty that I had decided to run away. But I couldn't help myself. Running away was in my blood. I just couldn't stay. I couldn't explain that. I couldn't stand staying with people for a long time. I couldn't stand getting attached. I felt like I had been trapped, or I had been in prison, or shackled.

Every girl I started dating was pretty and nice. Anyway, I was not a womanizer. I dated only few women. However, after I left my hometown I was almost always surrounded by nice people. But the moment I felt a girl started getting attached to me or I started having feelings for her, I would get scared. And I would leave her. Or I would just start avoiding her. It was not something that I really wanted but some animal instinct, something inborn or programmed in me pushed me to do that, to run away. And no matter how much I liked the girl, that feeling to run away, to break free, to be alone, unattached and uncommitted was stronger than anything else.

There was one girl that I particularly liked and loved. Her name was Silvia. We dated for a few months and I started feeling that I really liked her. As the time was passing by, we started seeing each other more often. But then she also started calling me almost every day, and I flipped. I couldn't stand that. I got scared and I started avoiding her. The more I avoided her, the more persistent she was. Silvia was leaving me messages that I never replied to. She was asking my friends if they had seen me. And then she even started waiting for me in front of my building. I was getting crazy and I decided to change the apartment. I rented a small apartment on the totally opposite side of the city from my previous place. I couldn't understand why she was so persistent. Couldn't she get it? How come she didn't realize that I didn't want to see her?! It took her few months to stop chasing me. When I started slowly forgetting her, one day, in a park, in the center of the city I saw her. And I was shocked. She was not the same! She was bigger, not fatter, just her stomach bulged. Silvia was pregnant! And it stuck me! She had been so persistent in talking to me and meeting me because she had wanted to tell me the news! I was frozen and couldn't move. I was just standing there and I knew she saw me and saw my shock. But she didn't come to me. She turned around and went in the opposite direction. I was probably standing there for more than half an hour with a lost face expression, since an older woman approached me and asked me if I needed some help.

The next few days I couldn't eat or sleep. I called my mother and I told her about the baby. She seemed not listening to my outcry for help. She was too excited that she would become a grandma. She was like a parrot repeating the same things over and over again: "Oh, Igor! It is amazing! It is wonderful! I will be a grandma!"

I had no one else to share my fear, anxiety, and confusion with. I was walking every day marathon distances hoping that these long walks would give me an answer what to do. I was sitting in a park watching children playing and no matter how funny and interesting they were, they were someone else's children. The fact that I would have my own child who would turn my life into a prison of fatherhood and family life, into some kind of bond, dependence, commitment, scared the crap out of me. On the other hand, how could I have been such an idiot and leave Silvia alone to raise a child?! One evening, I decided to go to Silvia's house and see her. I didn't find a solution for the whole situation and I didn't know what to do but I just wanted to see her. Before leaving my apartment I drank a few glasses of vodka. I needed alcohol to help me cope with that situation. When I came in front of Silvia's house, I stayed in front of it for 10 minutes thinking what to say and do. I still didn't figure it out. Then I knocked on her door. She opened the door and the wave of surprise hit her face. She was holding the door knob and probably hesitating if she should shut the door in my face or let me in.

Finally, she let me come in. I sat in a chair and asked her how she was. She didn't answer, just have me a scornful look. There was a moment of silence and then I began apologizing and telling her that

I was scared of commitments and attachments. I wanted to explain to her what it meant to me to get attached to someone. I really wanted to describe how hard it was for me, but I failed because the words couldn't describe it. She seemed ignorant to my explanation and somehow distant as if thinking about something else. When I stopped talking, because I understood that she didn't care for my words, she told me that I had no obligation to accept the child. She decided to take care of it alone. I was looking at her and Silvia seemed so cold while telling me that. I told her that I wanted to try to take care of it as well. I told her I was not sure if I could be a good father but that I was willing to try. She looked through the opened window and didn't say anything. After few minutes of complete silence, she told me she had to think about if she wanted me in her and her baby's life. I said "alright" and stood up from the chair to leave. While I was on the way to the door, she called me and told me that I had hurt her and she was not sure if she wanted to forgive me. I saw tears in her eyes and I felt awful. I told her I was sorry and I left. I was not sure what I was thinking when I told Silvia I would like to take care of baby as well. But I know that seeing her so fragile, distant, sad and lonely made me put some efforts to try not to run away. The next day, Silvia called me and said she had thought about what I had said and she wanted to try again. She said the baby would need a father and since I, Igor, was its biological father, she couldn't think about anyone better than me to take care of it. I was not sure if she was right. I knew nothing about babies and I was not sure I would fulfill the role of a father. But I said I would try, so I had to try.

After few days, Silvia moved to my apartment. It seemed strange to live with someone after so many years of loneliness. In the beginning, I couldn't stand the idea that I had to share my sacred place with her and going back home after work was a bit unpleasant, but after few weeks, I got used to. Silvia also put efforts not to disturb too much my daily routine, so she made sure not to be too present everywhere and she gave me a lot of space. She would prepare meals before I came back home and then retreat to the bedroom leaving me the spaciousness of living room. She knew I liked watching TV while lying down on a couch. She didn't talk much either. It seemed as if she had understood my weirdness, as if she had realized my deformity and tried to adjust herself to it and I loved her even more because of that. I started thinking that probably she was the only person who understood me. And it was not easy, since often I didn't understand myself.

Then, the big day came. Silvia had a long and difficult labor. It was a cesarean delivery. They had to cut her. But a baby girl was healthy and fine. We named her Dori. How did I feel? It was a mix of shock, or better terror, and happiness. Dori was crying all the time. She was purple and pretty ugly but there was something spectacular in the whole process of being a part of the creation of new life. And this baby girl was part of my blood, skin, cells. I didn't know how to behave in the hospital but I know that there was a smile on my face. And Silvia, my unwed wife was happy. I tried to hold Dori but my hands were shaking so after a minute I gave up.

After a week, when we brought Dori to our apartment, a new scary part of my life began. Dori was sleeping during the day and crying during the night. I tried to ignore her and let Silvia take care of her, but even her mother was struggling to calm her down. We had our nerves on edge. I couldn't stand listening to Dori crying. And I told Silvia I would spend some time in the hotel not that far from our apartment. She was upset and started accusing me of being a lousy father. She said she had known this would happen. I told her that would be only temporarily and that after few weeks, I would come back home. She said that the baby would not disappear after few weeks. And it was the end of our conversation.

My days in the hotel were like a holiday. It was a real vacation for me. And I couldn't stop thinking that for the last 9 months of my life with someone else I had lost myself. Only when I was alone did I feel alive and at peace with myself. Maybe I was not meant to share my life with anyone else.

These thoughts started harassing me and I stayed in the hotel much longer than I had initially planned. I spent 2 months there. Finally, I picked up courage to go back to the apartment. But the next days were unbearable. While before Dori was born, Silvia had done everything to make me feel comfortable in that apartment, this time, she was putting efforts to annoy me and piss me off. She was loud, sloppy and had some weird emotional outbursts. One moment, she was crying and the next she laughed like a maniac for no reason. I started feeling like a stranger in my own apartment. I tried to talk to her, but she seemed not willing to listen to me. She talked all the time, actually shouted and told me that I could leave any time because she didn't need me. And that's what I did.

One early morning, when both she and Dori were sleeping, I packed the necessary things I wanted to bring with me and I left. I didn't have plans, schedule, idea where I was going. I sat in my car and started driving. I left the city and continued toward the small town not that far. I found a cheap motel and stayed there two nights. Finally, I pulled myself together and started looking for jobs on the Internet. And I found one! In a foreign country, on the other continent! But that was what I needed and wanted: to run away from everything and everyone. I applied and after two days I got an answer. They scheduled me a Skype interview and I got the job! I was supposed to leave within three days. As far as I was concerned, I could have left the same moment they informed me I had got the job.

The morning before my departure, I called Silvia and I told her that I was leaving but that I would keep sending money for her and Dori every month. Silvia didn't want to talk and she didn't say even a word. She just hung up the phone.

I did what I had promised. Every month, I sent the same amount of money and I knew it was more than enough for the two of them to lead a normal life. And I also knew that the money couldn't make up for my absence from my daughter's life but I didn't know any better. I was a sad man with a strange deformity which was irreparable.

The new country, new climate, new language, new people. I got what I wanted. I was a complete stranger in a new place. No one to stifle me, to ask me to stay, to look for me. But my heart was heavy. I knew that I left my child. That thought forever cursed me. It tortured me. But I also knew that I would never be a good father. And I wished Silvia would find someone else who would be a decent father to Dori.

Few years passed and I never called them to ask how they were. Yes, I know. I was the last living bastard. Then, my cousin called me one day. He told me that my mother passed away. I was sad and I even felt like crying but my self-sufficiency taught me not to cry over anyone. I knew she had been probably the only person who had loved me the way I was and never tried to change me or judge me. And she died. I packed my backpack, booked the first flight and went to her funeral. I didn't spend the night in my hometown. Instead, I went to the city where I used to live and where my daughter now lived. Somehow, I believed and felt that the two of them still lived in the same apartment. And some strange curiosity, guilt and sorrow pushed me to walk the streets nearby. It was a sunny afternoon, and kids were playing in the park. I found an empty bench far from people and sat there watching the kids playing. Somehow I hoped I would see my daughter. Half an hour passed and I didn't see her. It was silly of me to think that she would just appear there because I wanted to see her. Finally, I stood up and started walking toward the bus station. And then, I saw them: Dori, who was a beautiful 5-year-old blonde girl in a purple dress, Silvia, who hadn't changed much and a man in a jeans and dark blue T-shirt. The three of them looked so happy. They seemed like a happy family coming back from the zoo or cinema. They were giggling and smiling. First, I was confused by the scene I had witnessed but then I felt some weird dose of happiness and comfort that the two of them were not alone, that they had the man who was able to take care of them. He was probably everything I was not able to be: a father, a husband, a lover. It made me even more deformed, since I couldn't believe that I was happy because some other man replaced me. What a weirdo and freak I was! But I was happy, indeed.

I went back to the country which then I called my home and I continued my simple hermit life of non-attachments, simplicity, quietness, loneliness and work.

Many many years passed. On my fiftieth birthday, I got a birthday card. The only birthday card I had received in the last 25 years. It was a shocking experience. Someone was thinking about me even if I didn't think much about anyone in particular. And probably the only person I thought about once in a while was my daughter but she probably didn't know that I existed. I doubted her mother told her about me. But I was wrong. The card was simple, with blue and white stripes and a small teddy bear who was holding a birthday present in his arms in the right corner of the card. It said:

"Happy birthday dad! Wishing you a lot of love and happiness!" I was holding it in my hand for who knows how long. I can't explain how I felt. I just know that unwanted tears started filling my eyes and when my eyes were not enough to hold all the tear flood, the tears started falling down on the birthday card and within a minute, the card was all wet and the letters smeared. I let the tears fall down and I sat in the chair with my face buried in my hands. I don't know how long I stayed in that position, but I know that when I finally stood up it was pitch dark outside. The rest of the day I spent drinking vodka, and when I was so drunk that I couldn't see anything in front of me except some blurred images, I guess I fell asleep. The next day was a working day and somehow I managed to pull myself together, take shower and decided to walk to my office. I had a bad hangover and didn't feel capable of driving a car. Even while I was walking, I still saw blurred images and my balance was not great. I was staggering, swaying a little and even though the thought of calling my boss and asking him to take a sick day crossed my mind, I didn't feel like spending a day in the apartment. So I decided to go to work anyway and somehow. I was going slowly since I couldn't walk fast. Then, something weird happened. I started having a headache. The pain in the right side of my head and whole body was getting more and more intense. It seemed that with every new breath the pain was getting stronger, and at one moment, I felt that it paralyzed the parts of my body. I wanted to ask someone for help but it seemed that I was not able to speak.

Actually, my muscles started getting weak and motionless, and the next thing I remember was blackness all around me.

I woke up in a hospital room. First, I didn't know where I was and it took me some time to remember who I was. My brain was working slowly. I couldn't remember many things: where from I was, what language I speak, how old I was. Somehow, it took me so long to remember these. I wished I had had a remote to speed up my brain. Then, I realized that I couldn't move my left arm and left leg. My left side seemed paralyzed. There was that sharp stabbing pain all around my chest and my vision was still a bit blurred. The doctor came and told me I had had a pretty bad stroke. He told me I couldn't talk and I had difficulties moving the left side of my body. Luckily, my right side was still fine. But he told me that I would have to spend some time in hospital since they were afraid that my condition could get worse. They were afraid that I might have another stroke and wanted to monitor my condition. Since I couldn't talk, the doctor asked me to write down if I needed anything. And he left me a notebook and a pen. I didn't know what I was feeling. I guess I felt pain and numbness at the same time. And I felt like crying but for some reason the tears wouldn't fall down. I was all alone and I asked myself: wasn't that what I had always wanted? To be left alone. Well, I got it! I didn't have anyone to be there with me and I didn't want anyone I knew to see me in that condition. But I couldn't stop thinking about Dori. Actually, she was the only one I wished had been there. However, I would have never called her. I would not like her to see me and meet me in that condition. However, I felt that I owed her explanation of who her biological father was, how he felt, how he grew up, how he ran away from everything and everyone constantly through his life. I wanted her to know all that. So I took the notebook and the pen and I started writing. I couldn't write fast. I was writing maybe half a page per day, and here I am now still writing but finally finishing what I wanted her to know. My hands are shaking and I am so happy that I have managed to more or less write everything I wanted to tell her. And again, maybe some parts are not very well-written and I am not sure she will understand how I have felt my whole life, I am afraid that she will not understand my deformity, my devious character, my distortions. But I honestly hope she will. That is the only thing that comforts me. And I feel that I will probably not be here for long and that is not at all a scary thing. What scares me is that Dori will never find out that I love her. And I have always loved her in my weird way. Maybe I have never been a normal human being but my feelings for her are as strong as any father could have for a child. Maybe even stronger. No matter that this father failed as the father, he has always loved his daughter.

A Tomboy

Vera's mother, Mrs. Schmidt, suddenly entered the house, slamming the door as always. Her fierce movements, noise that she made, and loud talk, always disturbed Vera's peacefulness. This time, Mrs. Schmidt approached the kitchen table at which Vera was sitting and eating a bowl of cereals, and placed the book "How to Awaken the Divine Feminine within You" on the table in front of Vera.

"What's this?" Vera cried irritated and shocked.

"Well, dear, I think it is really important that you start doing something with your life. Look at you!

Twenty-two years old and still wearing some baggy T-shirt, two sizes bigger jeans and white socks!

Disaster! And look at your hair! An absolute mess! As if someone had put fireworks in it. I am not surprised you can't find a boyfriend. No decent young man wants to date a tomboy."

Mrs. Schmidt turned around and went out through the kitchen door toward her bedroom leaving the strong fragrance of flowery perfume behind her.

For many years, Mrs. Schmidt had tried to help her daughter wake up her femininity and find a proper boyfriend or any boyfriend at all. She was afraid Vera would become a spinster. Old, ugly, alone. She couldn't accept that her daughter was so much different than her. Mind you, her father had been exactly the same. Even though, he had passed away when Vera was only two years old, he embedded his character and behavior in her for good. But what she didn't know was that Vera had a boyfriend. And Vera's decision not to tell her was reasonable. Her mother would never accept Frank. Vera met Frank when she was watching a local football match. Every Sunday one of two local football teams were playing on the only stadium in Blanktown. Vera loved football and she was also the member of the local female football team. Anyway, Blankville was a small place and there was not much to do. Kids and young people played tennis, football, volleyball or they rode bicycles. Vera loved not only football. She loved rugby, baseball, wrestling, boxing. Those were the sports not many girls enjoyed, but Vera was a unicorn. She wore baggy clothes, a bit over-sized but comfortable. She felt fine in those loose-fitting clothing pieces. Hew jeans were roomy, but they had never made her sweat and feel confined. Her large T-shirts didn't exaggerate her ample breast and didn't attract much attention as they would have done if she had worn tight clothes. Vera had a beautiful long blonde hair. Her hair fell loosely to her waist. She had never gone to a hair salon, and she had never used hair sprays, hair gels and hair wax to make her hair look differently than it was.

She liked it long and loose. And even though, it always looked plain and simple, the absence of a hairstyle suited her well. Her big blue eyes gave her a soft, timid look. They had an ocean-color hue which made them special. Her Roman nose was a bit large for her oval face but it didn't destroy her exquisitely imperfect beauty.

The first time Frank saw her on the football stadium, the first thing he noticed were her eyes and nose. He found them so appealing and matching that he couldn't think of ever seeing the facial features more analogous to the epitome of perfection. For him, she was perfect the way she was.

When he saw her that first time, she was sitting in the first row, just behind the football players' bench. Of course, he had to be there as well. He didn't have a choice. There, close to the first row, was the only area for people with disabilities. And he was the one. He was wheelchair bound. Once upon a time, more than ten years ago, he had used to play football. He had been a good player, a striker. But after the car accident, in which his older brother had died, he had been not only left brotherless but legless as well. Actually, he had legs but they were useless. Their uselessness made him handicapped, or better said, disabled, how certain people talked about him trying not to offend him. Anyway, he had been already offended. Not by people, but by life itself. There were days when he pitied himself and there were days when he hated his wheelchair, his idle legs and everything that made him stranded in the middle of inactivity. For a sportsman, and he had been a committed one, that was the biggest punishment.

When Frank saw Vera, for a moment, he forgot that he was in the wheelchair. He forgot that he was not an ordinary guy, who could casually approach a girl, sit next to her and start a conversation. He looked at her and his body started moving as if he would start walking. But while his chest, and his heart that was beating loudly, and his eyes that were fixed on the place where Vera was sitting, moved forward, his legs stayed glued to the wheel chair. He looked down at his useless legs and muttered: "Damn it!" However, Frank didn't want to give up on this girl. Maybe some other girl would discourage him with her stern face, unapproachable attitude and ignorance, but Vera gave him the feeling of easygoingness which she radiated and her omnipresent smile showed him that she celebrated not only the goals during the football match but life itself. It all encouraged him to place his hands on the wheels of his wheelchair and let the chair roll toward Vera. When he came just next to her seat, and luckily, she was at the very end of the row, which made it possible for him to place himself next to her, he started the small talk. She was friendly and accepted this casual chitchat with a stranger, who was, by the way, an innocuous-looking man. They talked and watched the game, and after the game they exchanged phone numbers. That was how their relationship had started.

As the weeks went by, Vera started thinking how to tell her mother that she was seeing someone. There was not an easy way. Her mother desperately wanted her to find a boyfriend but Frank didn't fit in her mother's ideal of a proper man. No matter that her mother was a member of Blanktown Spirit Club which provided funding support for mobility devices for people with disabilities, and she probably had helped Frank get his wheelchair, she would doubtless not be able to accept Frank as her daughter's boyfriend. Her criteria used to approve Vera's boyfriend included "ability to walk", and Frank failed there. But Blanktown was a small place and sooner or later her mother would find out. Vera preferred telling her directly than waiting her mother to hear the shocking news from some gossip ladies.

The day when Mrs. Schmidt threw the book "How to Awaken the Divine Feminine within You" on the table in front of Vera was probably the good day for Vera to tell her the news. She finished her bowl of cereals, breathed in nervously, stood up, walked to the door of her mother's bedroom and knocked on it.

Mrs. Schmidt yelled: "Come in."

When Vera entered her mother's bedroom, she found her mother lying in bed with pink hair rollers in her hair which were supposed to make her hair curly. She had been obviously reading a book, but she let it on her nightstand when Vera entered the room. Vera sat on the edge of the bed and just said it without introduction: "I've been seeing Frank lately."

"Frank who?" Her mother was surprised.

"Frank Marley." Vera said in a shaky voice.

Her mother's eyes were wide open in surprise and bulging out of her head as if she had just seen a ghost. Then, silence followed. To Vera, those moments of silence seemed like eons. Her mother took back her book from the nightstand and continued reading. Or she just pretended that she was reading. Vera noticed that her hands were trembling and she got slight head jerks from the shock and probably anger.

Vera stood up realizing that the conversation was over without any outcome, happy or bad. But probably it would have been bad, knowing her mother, if Vera had insisted on talking. Vera preferred not to push her mother over the edge of her temper. The next few days, Mrs. Schmidt avoided talking to her daughter. Actually, she avoided Vera.

She would leave before Vera woke up and come back home when Vera was not there. As if she had had spies around the house who had told her when her own daughter hadn't been at home.

Vera knew the silence wouldn't last forever and what she feared was that once that silence was broken it would be shattered into pieces with the fiercest shrapnel of words which would storm out of her mother's mouth. When finally, that day arrived it was even worse than Vera had expected.

One afternoon, six days after Vera had revealed the unpleasant truth, Mrs. Schmidt came back home earlier than usual and found Vera at home. Her piled up anger burst out immediately she saw her daughter and she said some bad things. She told Vera that she preferred her remaining single until the rest of her life and staying a tomboy without attracting men's attention than dating a crippled man. She told her that she would not have a nice future with Frank. She told her that she would have to take care of him and that she would be obliged to become a "handicapped man's maid". And she told her that she, as her mother, couldn't accept that her daughter married an invalid. She told her that she would have to choose between her mother and Frank, and that if she chose Frank, she should leave the house immediately.

Vera couldn't believe what she had just heard. She didn't believe her mother would go so far and say those terrible things. She knew her mother had a weird temper but while listening to those awful things she had just said, she for a moment thought of her mother as an evil witch. She started crying, ran to her room, packed few things in her backpack and ran out of the house weeping. She didn't choose either Frank or her own mother. It was such a cruel thing her mother had asked her to do. But she chose not to live in the same house with this woman she couldn't recognize anymore.

That night she stayed in her friend's place and the very next morning she saw Frank and told him everything. Frank was shocked and hurt. He didn't know what to say or do, but he offered Vera to stay in his house. He wanted to see her smile again.

Vera first refused since he lived in a small house with his parents and grandma. And even with only Frank's family, the house was cramped. She didn't feel comfortable to make it over- cramped. But Frank promised her that it would be just a temporary solution for the next few days until they made a better plan. And that was the truth. He believed that their future looked bright.

After a week of the unpleasant incident, Frank got a job offer in Bloomville. It was a town around nine hundred miles from Blanktown. He was offered a position of sports counselor in a big athletic company which sold football equipment as well as strength and athletic training products. It was a great opportunity for Frank. He offered Vera to move there together and to start a new life.

Even though, Vera was confused and a bit surprised by this offer, she was happy for Frank and felt that she could share her life with this man. It didn't mean that she chose him over her mother, since she didn't want there to be any choice, but she just felt comfortable in his company and didn't want to go back to her mother's place and her mother's constant preaching, especially, after everything Mrs. Schmidt had said.

Within a week, Vera and Frank moved to Bloomville. Frank seemed pretty excited because of the job offer. And he was honestly grateful for the opportunity. Realistically, not many companies offered this kind of positions to people with disabilities. Frank believed he was the lucky one. He thanked his lucky stars. However, he was even happier that Vera had decided to join him. He was growing fonder of her. Since he had met her, things had seemed going well for him. She was his lucky charm.

Vera was pretty excited about the prospect and because of moving to the other town. She was ready for change in her life. It enlivened her mood. But the worm of worry wriggled in her mind. She was hurt by her mother's words and she knew her mother would not make an attempt to bury the hatchet and make up with Vera. Mrs. Schmidt was the woman of principles and no matter how bad those principles were, she didn't want to give up on them. She faithfully followed them like every old-fashioned woman and even if she realized she had made a mistake, she had never apologized. For her, women were meant to be ladies, to embrace and cherish their femininity and wear it as a halo. They were supposed to be gentle, subtle but strong-minded and educated.

Tomboys were outcasts of those feminine circles. And Mrs. Schmidt could not accept the fact that her own daughter had accepted to be an outcast. The culmination of her disappointment in her own daughter was when she started dating a handicapped man. Women were meant to be taken care of, and the men were father figures, head of the families and strong and capable creatures with all limbs perfectly mobile. And what had her daughter decided? To be a maid to an invalid! Mrs. Schmidt couldn't accept this. Somehow, all those years she had been struggling to accept her daughter's tom- boyishness, but this was unacceptable! She loved her daughter and the fact that she was not even a little like her was breaking her heart. She felt more estranged from her daughter than ever.

Vera didn't want to apologize to her mother because she thought there was nothing to apologize for. But she felt the need to tell her mother that she was moving to the other town.

However, Vera was not ready yet to meet her mother. Fresh wounds still hurt her. A day before she left, she had written a short note to her mother informing her about her life change. Vera left the note in the mailbox of their house when her mother was not at home. It might have been a cowardly act but she preferred being a coward in this case than facing another outburst of her mother's anger. Bloomville was a nice little town. There were the headquarters of few big companies and Frank's company was one of them. During the first two months, Vera and Frank were still settling down in the new town, getting used to the new environment and new people. Vera didn't give up on her baggy T-shirts and jeans and no one seemed to care about it. Bloomville seemed a bit less conservative town than Blanktown. Frank loved his job and after six months of proving that he was a good choice the company's bosses made, Frank came back home to Vera, one Tuesday evening, with the news that his bosses were interesting in interviewing her for the position of assistant marketing manager. The job description, as Frank assured her, completely suited her. And maybe it was not her dream job, but finding a job was one of her priorities since she started feeling lonely and useless while Frank was at work. Frank's salary was more than enough for the two of them, but she wanted to work.

The job interview requested formal clothes, so she had to put up with the pants, shirt and blazer. She liked the interviewers and they liked her. The job was hers! Simple as that! Vera and Frank led a calm life. They worked from nine to five, sometimes a bit longer, spent evenings cooking food, eating it, drinking wine, watching movies and playing cards. Once in a while, they would go out for a beer with the colleagues from work. Two years went by and they decided that it was time to end the relationship and start a married life. They planned a small wedding with Frank's parents and grandma, colleagues from work and hopefully Mrs. Schmidt.

However, that was something Vera feared. After two years of not talking to her mother, she was not sure how to approach her and how to invite her to the wedding. She doubted her mother would attend it, but she was ready to talk to her and ask the honor of her presence.

One Sunday morning, when she was sure her mother was at home, eating her poached eggs and toast while watching her favorite family show on TV, Vera picked up the phone and called her. She didn't prepare any speech and she didn't want a long conversation. She was not sure her mother even wanted to talk to her. After few rings, her mother picked up the phone. Vera was sure she didn't expect to hear her daughter's voice. And she was right. Mrs. Schmidt was shocked. But she pretended that she was not. On Vera's "good morning, mother", she just irritatingly signed and said "good morning". After ten second of silence which seemed much longer, she asked Vera:

"What is the reason for this phone call?"

"I am getting married mother. And I would love you to be there." Vera assuredly said. Mrs. Schmidt didn't say anything for a long time. Maybe even the whole minute without words passed and Vera finally picked up the courage to say something: "Mother?"

"No, I can't attend your wedding. Good bye, Vera." Her mother said in a low voice. Vera was not very surprised. Whatsoever, she expected something like this. What was surprising was the long silence after Vera's invitation. It seemed as if Vera's mother had been taking into consideration the option of attending her daughter's wedding. Maybe that was the proof that her mother had softened up a bit. But Vera had no proofs to believe that.

The wedding ceremony was simple but beautiful. Vera was happy, but not completely. She felt lonely. There was no one from her family to attend the wedding. She was the loneliest girl on her own wedding. And the sparks of sadness flared within her. But no one seemed to notice that.

Maybe only Frank. He kept holding her hand in his, spreading his cozy warmth through her body.

She was grateful he was doing that. She was certain he was the man of her dreams.

However, Vera didn't give up on her mother. The day after the wedding ceremony, she put few wedding photos in an envelope and send them to Mrs. Schmidt. She might throw them away but Vera felt the need to show her that she was happy and that she was lonely during her own wedding day, with no one from her family to walk her down the aisle and to be by her side. The married life was the same like the unmarried one. Nothing had changed. Vera and Frank continued their lovely routine and whenever they went together they set the example of the perfect couple, smiling, holding hands and giggling to each other's jokes.

Three years went by and Vera hadn't heard from her mother. And one Saturday night at eleven when both Vera and Frank were getting ready to go to bed, a phone ringed. They looked at each other and confused expressions crossed their faces. Vera took the receiver and heard the well- know deep voice of her neighbor back in Blanktown, and a friend of her mother, Mrs. Winterbottom. Mrs. Winterbottom apologized for calling so late but sadly she had unfortunate news that couldn't wait until morning. Vera's face froze after hearing this and she knew that something was wrong with her mother. Mrs. Winterbottom confirmed Vera's suspicions. She told Vera that her mother had had a heart attack that afternoon and that she was in hospital unconscious. The doctors didn't know what to expect next and they had confirmed that her mother's condition had been critical. Mrs. Winterbottom asked Vera to come to Blanktown as soon as possible. Vera, of course, confirmed that she would be there the very next day and she thanked Mrs. Winterbottom for letting her know.

After hearing the bad news, Vera felt like crying. And she couldn't and didn't want to hold the tears. She let them fall down her cheeks, salty and heavy, and she gave vent to all those repressed emotions connected to her mother and their fight, which had piled up through years and bothered the very soul of hers. She cried for almost an hour, holding Frank's hand and not letting it. She was scared, scared of losing her mother, who, hard and stubborn as she was, was her only mother.

That night she couldn't sleep at all. She and Frank talked until one in the morning and then, they just laid in bed hugging each other and reassuring each other that everything would be all right.

At four in the morning they stood up, having not slept at all, put the clothes on and headed to the train station to catch the first train to Blanktown. It was a long trip. It took them eighteen hours to reach Blanktown. They arrived to their hometown just before midnight. And unfortunately, they were late.

Mrs. Schmidt had passed away at ten in the morning that day. Her heart muscle had been badly damaged as well as all other vital organs, and after some time her heart had failed. Vera and Frank were devastated, especially Vera, who hadn't managed to see her mother before she had died and try to make peace with her. She wanted to tell her so many things, and she wanted to start all over again their mother-daughter relationship, but it was late now. She didn't even have tears to shed since the previous night she had cried a river.

Vera and Frank stayed in the old Frank's house with his family and early in the morning next day, Vera decided to go to her house alone. Frank knew she needed to be alone for a while and calm down her disturbed mind. He didn't insist on making her company.

When Vera came to the front yard of her house, she stood still there reminiscing about her own childhood. She had been a happy child, a tomboy, an outcast as her mother had called her. Her mother had had a real temper and there had been disagreements between them, but they also had spent some great times together. Vera remembered all those short trips to the zoo, entertainment water parks, coastline snorkeling excursions, botanical gardens. Those had been the best parts of her childhood. And during those trips her mother had been her best friend. That Mrs. Schmidt was the one Vera would always remember.

After few minutes of digesting all those memories and trying to put them in a proper order, Vera entered the house. Everything looked the same as it had been many years ago. Chairs, table, lamps, curtains. Except one thing. In the living room, on the small table with a flower pot and the old black home dial phone, next to the phone receiver, there was a photo from the Vera and Frank's wedding, the one that Vera had sent to her mother. On that photo, Vera and Frank were both smiling looking at each other instead at the camera and they seemed very happy. Vera came closer to the small table and took the photo. She held it in her hands for few moments and then again, she felt that the warm tears started gathering in the corners of her eyes. Her mother had probably accepted the fact that her daughter had loved and married a man with a disability. She had probably forgiven Vera for not being the girl she had wanted her to be. And she had probably loved her and missed her as much as Vera loved and missed her mother. Few tears ran down Vera's face and fell on the glass frame of the photo. Vera wiped the glass and squeezed it in her hands. She sat in the chair next to the window looking outside and thought how sometimes life didn't bring back people to each other but death. And even though she was sad, she knew that her mother had forgiven her. And that was a relief. She had forgiven her for being more different than alike. And what she read on the back side of the photo that probably her mother had written before she had framed the photo, just confirmed Vera's thoughts:

"The heart of a mother is a deep abyss at the bottom of which you will always find forgiveness." - Honore de Balzac

And Vera? Vera had forgiven her mother a long time ago.

Mr. Madman's House

Everyone in Klonville knew him as Mr. Madman. His real name was Hank, but rarely anyone knew it.

Mr. Madman was a strange creature. He was probably in his late forties. He was tall and had pretty messy shoulder-length hair, beard that always looked dirty, very thick eyebrows that almost met in the middle above the bridge of the nose and long, broad and upright ears resembling ones of a vampire. He had broad shoulders, strong arms, very big hands that could probably pull up a smaller tree together with its roots. His legs were long and his feet large. His appearance alone was enough to scare not only children but grown-ups as well.

Mr. Madman lived alone in the house on the hill not so far from the town's cemetery. That fact even more emphasized his strangeness. And definitely, it provoked people to make up a lot of strange stories about him. However, it was not the only reason for those weird stories.

Mr. Madman had never got married. No woman wanted to marry such a strange man and he didn't seem interested in getting married and having a family. He had all those strange animals in his house and that was probably enough for him. Older people in Klonville remembered his mother who had been a very nice woman. She had been a writer and had rarely left the house. And when she had left it, she would go to the town's library to borrow some books or buy some groceries in the local shop. She had always wished a good day to everyone with a broad smile and had known everyone's name in the town. She had raised her son alone and no one had known or found out who the father of the child had been.

Mr. Madman was the peculiar child. He was an introvert boy who didn't play with the other kids. Instead, he collected animals and played with them. He had the whole menagerie of them. He always had either a frog, a lizard, a snail or a snake in his pocket. And his backpack was a temporary home to mice, squirrels, grasshoppers or crickets. Other kids stayed away from him but they didn't dare to bully him since he was much taller and stronger than any other boy his age.

He didn't talk almost at all. The teachers kept trying again and again to make him talk and answer their questions but every time he was asked about anything, he would just stare at the black board absentmindedly with an incomprehensible facial expression. No one could guess what he was thinking about. However, he loved reading books and he wrote some nice essays, but he would never read those essays aloud in front of the teacher and other kids in the classroom.

Once in a while, Mr. Madman would bring a frog or a snail into the classroom and let it rest on his desk. The teachers protested and other kids disgustingly frowned. But no reprimands and punishments discouraged him from bringing his pets to the classroom.

After he had finished the elementary school, no high school authorities wanted him as a student. And his schooling ended there. He started working on a local farm planting and picking up fruits and vegetables. This job didn't require talking and interacting with other employees. And Mr. Madman was a hard worker, a real asset, so his boss appreciated him.

Mr. Madman led a quiet life. After work, he would go back home, and probably spend time with his animals. No one knew how many of them he had. After his mother had passed away, no one entered his house. There were rumors that he had a room full of snakes, and that he slept with a piton in his bed. And some ladies heard from some other ladies in Klonville that during the night he visited cemetery and holding snakes in his hands, he sat on the tombs and hummed some strange creepy tunes. There were so many other stories about Mr. Madman and his house. There was a great deal of speculation about what was in his house. All those strange stories provoked not only children's but grown-ups' imagination as well.

One autumn day, a group of kids, bored with the same games they played every day, made a plan to break into Mr. Madman's house while he was at work. There were four of them, all of them ten or eleven years old. Tobby was the only one who didn't like the idea and he tried to persuade the others that this mischief was a bad game. He was not scared of what they might find in Mr. Madman's house, but he felt sorry for this man whom everyone either avoided or abhorred. He didn't do anything bad to anyone and he didn't deserve that kind of treatment.

Other curious children didn't let Tobby in peace. They teased him and blamed him for being a coward. Finally, Tobby gave in and decided to join them in their mischief.

The kids waited Mr. Madman to go to work. They were hiding in the bushes not that far from the house. Tobby reluctantly agreed to do his duty but he told them he would just take a look inside the house and leave. The kids made a plan to break the window and enter through it. The one overlooking the front porch was the easiest target. When they were sure that Mr Madman had left the house and turned around the corner, they waited another five minutes just to make sure he was far and couldn't hear the window breaking. Then, they cautiously emerged from their hiding place and approached the house. The tallest boy, Fabian, grabbed a rock and threw it at the window. And when all of them started cleaning the window pane from the broken glass pieces and getting ready to jump inside, they heard the fallen leaves rustling and someone's footsteps. They turned around and what they saw left them totally flabbergasted. It was Mr. Madman holding a big snake and standing still just a few steps far from them. He must have heard the window breaking! But that snake he was holding! The huge man and scary snake were the terrifying scene.

The kids started running toward the bushes they had been hiding in previously. Only Tobby remained standing not sure what to do. Mr. Madman didn't approach him. Instead, he slowly headed toward the front door of his house dragging his feet as if he had been very tired. He waved Tobby signaling to follow him. Tobby was not scared. He recognized in Mr. Madman's gestures the signs of friendliness.

Tobby was overwhelmed by the burst of excitement, anxiety and curiosity. And that curiosity didn't leave room for fear. He followed Mr. Madman to the inside of the house. When he entered the living room, Tobby's jaw dropped. He was so surprised by what he had found there that he couldn't speak.

In the middle of the room, there was a big aquarium full of colorful fish. Small in size, those beautiful fish swarmed all over the aquarium. Their swimming and moving graciously through the water was so beautiful that Tobby thought he could sit and watch them for hours. However, there were so many other distractions in the room, so Tobby couldn't just sit and watch the fish. In one corner of the living room, there was a small terrarium with three lizards. Two of them were green and the third one was black with white spots. There was moss, pebbles, small plants and soil inside their home. It looked cozy and comfortable for the lizards. Then, next to the lizards' terrarium, there was another one, almost the same size. This terrarium was a home to many insects. Tobby recognized springtails and millipedes, but there were some other insects he had never seen before.

Few meters far from the insects' terrarium, there was a huge bowl with tiny turtles. There were at least dozens of turtles. They seemed pretty happy swimming around water grass in their big home. Finally, after Tobby moved from the turtles' aquarium, he spotted the last glass container which was the biggest one, and it was empty. He turned around and looked at Mr. Madman who was standing in one corner of the living room still holding the big brown snake. Its body was wrapped around Mr. Madman's right hand. Mr. Madman nodded approvingly showing that that terrarium belonged to the snake and he said "Jo" revealing the snake's name. Then, he approached this big terrarium and placed Jo inside.

Mr. Madman retreated to the kitchen. It was a small room with no animals inside but there were a lot of books and magazines on the kitchen table. He didn't talk. Except introducing Jo to Tobby he didn't say a word the whole time. He put the kettle on the stove and obviously wanted to make tea.

Tobby sat in one of the kitchen's chairs and waited patiently. After a couple of minutes, Mr. Madman placed a cup of mint tea in front of Tobby. An increasingly strong mint fragrance filled the kitchen. Tobby's nostrils opened up with pleasure breathing in and letting the alluring scent fill his lungs.

The friendliness and hospitality of Mr. Madman made him feel ashamed of what he and his friends had done and attempted to do. Tobby felt the need to apologize for the mischief.

"I am really sorry for everything. Actually, I have never liked the idea of breaking into your house.

I'm sorry." Tobby said.

Mr. Madman could read the sincere look in Tobby's eyes. He just nodded his head in acknowledgment. He didn't say anything.

After a few minutes, when he finished sipping his tea, Tobby asked Mr. Madman if he could again take a look around the living room. Mr. Madman again nodded.

Tobby went back to the living room and moved from one glass container to the other investigating their inhabitants curiously and admiring them. He spent half an hour inspecting the animals in this magical room and then he heard Mr. Madman approaching him. Mr. Madman carried his working uniform indicating that he had to go to work. Tobby realized he had to leave. He reluctantly headed to the door and while leaving the porch he turned around and asked Mr. Madman if he could come back again the next day. Mr. Madman again just nodded his head "yes". Tobby smiled and finally left.

That afternoon, unfortunately, a bunch of policemen invaded Mr. Madman's house and everything changed for Mr. Madman and his animals. Tobby would learn that evening that his visit to Mr. Madman's house would not be possible the following day.

When Tobby's friends ran away that same day from Mr. Madman's yard, they went directly to the police station. They yelled and cried and told the whole story to the officers. The officers first didn't believe them. They called their parents and they also called Tobby's parents who was missing, by the way, and they realized that the kids' story might be true, since they reported that Mr. Madman had captured their friend Tobby and had probably tortured him. After a couple hours of writing the report and investigating the frightened kids, four policemen, armed with guns, went to check Mr. Madman's property. After they had checked the front yard and made sure no one was there they knocked on the door and found no answer. They broke in. There was no one inside except the animals in the living room. And all their glass homes and all those creatures shocked the policemen. Especially Jo, who was a big guy. The policemen called the special unit and some other animal experts and they confiscated all the animals. Some of the animals were released while Jo, the turtles, and the fish ended up in the capital's zoo. That same afternoon, some strange governmental officers came to the farm where Mr. Madman worked and took him to the mental asylum. He would never again see his animals or his house.

When Tobby came back home after spending some time in Mr. Madman's house, he found his grandmother immersed in worry. When she saw him safe and sound, she hugged him and started crying. Immediately, she called his parents who were in the police station being investigated about their son who had gone missing. Once they arrived home accompanied with the police officer, Tobby told them the whole truth skipping the part about the animals. The grown-ups didn't seem convinced. The other kids' story was so dramatic that they suspected Mr. Madman had drugged him and threatened him not to tell the truth. They sent him to the hospital for medical check-up. Tobby protested but to no avail.

Later that day, the doctors confirmed that there were no traces of any drugs in Tobby's body. There were no signs of any violence on his body either. He was released from hospital but still no one seemed to believe his story. He was repeating that Mr. Madman was a harmless sort of man and that he seemed a nice person but no one heard what he was saying. The grown-ups seemed so engaged in the drama spread all around Klonville that they didn't want to hear the truth. The drama was more interesting and they tended to keep it going until it reached its culmination. The animals just proved them that Mr. Madman was insane and that he needed to be in a special institution, locked and under supervision.

The kids' story, exaggerated and with the key facts misstated, brought too much attention.

Not only local newspapers, but national also, covered the story. And all of those stories had Mr. Madman as an anti-hero, villain and wrongdoer. What did he do to carry those titles? Everyone in Klonville had an opinion about it. And Tobby was probably the only one who knew him more than the others, even though, he spent only a couple of hours with him. But he couldn't help him. He was taken away, confined in some tiny depressive room, maybe he was even put in shackles. All those thoughts roamed Tobby's mind. But he was only ten years old and no one listened to him. No one believed him. He was only a kid.

As the weeks and months went by, people in Klonville started forgetting the whole episode with Mr. Madman and his animals. His house was abandoned and its walls and roof were slowly crumbling.

Many things disappeared from the house. The cutlery, furniture, TV, stove, radio. Only books and magazines remained. And they were being heavily damaged by humidity and neglect. Tobby managed to save few of them. A couple of times, he sneaked out and went there carefully not to be seen by anyone.

He was sad to see Mr. Madman's house in the state of dilapidation. And he wanted to have some memory of him. So, he took few of his books. He was afraid he would forget him the same way the other people in Klonville had done during the time. After the last visit to Mr. Madman's house remnants, he got an idea how to keep him in his memory forever. He went home and wrote a story about Mr. Madman.

Stefania's Little Secrets

From all the towns in the world, if she was asked to choose where she would like to live, Stefania would choose Buskagrad. Not because of the location. It was in the middle of a vast country with no coastline hundreds of miles around. It was not the most developed town. There were few big companies' offices and a big winery. And it didn't have a university. Therefore, those who wanted higher education went to the town thirty miles far, called Beovar, where they could enroll some of the courses at the University of Organizational Sciences. Buskagrad was not the most beautiful town in the country. There were no important historical and cultural buildings. The weather was not the best. Winters were cold and summers too hot. The people were narrow-minded like in every town. They lived of gossips and scandals and watched telenovelas. However, Stefania liked it. She loved Buskagrad because this town kept her secrets. This town never intruded into her past and never was too curious what it had looked like. Maybe because that not very nice past was the past of a small child. And no one believed that the small child remembered with the understanding the events that had marked her early childhood.

Stefania was an orphan. An older couple, Mr. and Mrs. Kupinovski, adopted her when she was five.

Before that, she had lived in the orphanage on the outskirts of Buskagrad for a year. And before that, she didn't want to remember that period of her life. Those years before she had ended up in the orphanage had been a nightmare and she feared the very thought of them. But in Buskagrad, no one really cared and asked about a little child's early childhood. However, the kids from the orphanage were different. They wanted to know everything. They were so curious. Hungry to find out if someone else's past had been more interesting and crueler than their own. And then, once they had the information, the story, they used it against the person who had revealed it.

Also the orphanage caregivers, psychologists and social workers were cruel in their aim to help the children. They asked too much and infringed upon the little children's private scary memories. But since she claimed she didn't remember anything, they eventually let her be. Was it a truth? No. It was the biggest lie she had ever told. Actually, she remembered everything. Those memories were so vivid that even she was confused how it was possible to remember everything to the smallest details.

She was an illegitimate child. Her biological mother was a drunkard and when she was drunk she didn't have much control of what she did. She slept with random men. A man would invite her for dinner, pay for it. She was bored and intoxicated and she slept with the man. That was the unromantic truth about her sexual hookups. Stefania didn't know who her father was and probably her mother hadn't known either.

They lived in an old building, on the second floor. It was a shabby one-bedroom apartment overlooking the train rails. The building was in the industrial part of the town and factories' sirens, train horns, trucks, cars and other vehicles made a lot of noise, night and day. For a child, that noise was not that unbearable, but grownups were getting crazy. The building inhabitants were drunkards, junkies, aggressive men and loose women, wanton seductresses and pimps. The children, the unfortunate offspring of the outcast parents, were roaming around, stealing food from the local shops and markets and sleeping on the park benches when their parents got mad and their behavior turned into aggression or violence.

Stefania was not one them. Her mother would lock her in the apartment, often without food, and Stefania would spend a day or two hungry, playing with her two rag dolls. The dolls were so old that their body parts were missing and their dirty doll dresses were all in pieces. But she still loved them. They were her only companions in those lonely hungry hours. And they helped her not to think about the food. They kept her occupied. Her mother would usually appear after a day or two and bring a plastic bag with some groceries, alcohol bottles and cigarettes. Wasted as she was most of the time, she would go to sleep and leave the bag on the table. Stefania who was starving would often take whatever she found eatable in the bag. Some-times, an apple, bread, orange, peanuts, or a half-eaten sand-wich that her mother hadn't finished. She would devour ev-erything that was food or looked like. She was so hungry that she thought she could eat even the cigarettes if only they didn't taste so bad. And when finally, after a few-hours-long nap her mother woke up and checked the content of the bag she had brought, she would find only her alcohol and cigarettes. If she was sober after the long nap and in a good mood, she would say nothing. But if the nap didn't make her clear- headed and if alcohol still ran though her body, she would get mad at Ste-fania. A slap or two were not enough. She lit a cigarette. The pungent smell filled the air. She smoked fast and then, out of blue, she burned the cigarette on Stefania's skin. Some kind of twisted smile was on her face when she was doing it. It was a demonic smile, frantic and wild. Even her eyes were the eyes of a devil in those moments, and Stefania feared the way they looked at her as if they wanted to penetrate her eyes and take them out of her eyeballs, to remove them from their sockets. Stefania cried loudly and wanted to run away. But there was no place to run and hide. Her mother would grab her and with a new cigarette just lit, again burn her skin. After few cigarettes, she would stop and retreat to bed. Stefania cried. Big tears rolled down her dirty cheeks and wetted her old T-shirt that smelled like sweat and tears. Her arms, legs and shoulders were marked with cigarette burns. Those were the marks she would wear all her life as a memory to the secrets that she wanted to bury. But she couldn't bury them. They were too visible.

In Buskagrad, and in her new home, no one asked about how those marks had appeared. Her foster parents probably knew but they didn't torture her with questions. They didn't want to remind her of that hell of a life, and they didn't know if she still remembered. They thought that probably such a small child forgot the unfortunate events. But how could you forget those things?

Martha, her foster mother, and Tomas, her foster father, were worried that she was not able to talk when they adopted her. Even though, the social workers from the orphanage and other workers there confirmed that she had been talking, not much though, Martha and Tomas had their fears and they believed that Stefania's refusal to speak was her rejection to talk about the past. They agreed never to ask her about anything that had happened when she had still lived with her biological mother, that poor wicked creature who had sponged alcohol and sunk in debauchery. However, they asked for a professional help. A lovely lady, whose name was Fiona, and who was an expert for children's social disorders helped Stefania to get back her wish to talk. Fiona's patience, games and heaps of smiles gave some unusual comfort to the little girl and Stefania started talking again. Not much though, but at least she talked. Fiona had become not only a friend to the little girl but a guardian angel. The little girl looked up at her and admired her way of talking, her graceful movements, her childish games and stories she read to Stefania. Even after the official treatment ended, she continued visiting Mr. and Mrs. Kupinovski and little Stefania. And she also didn't insist on knowing about the events from Stefania's past. Stefania's secrets were safely buried in her own memory. And she preferred keeping them there. She was fine with never letting them out.

The image that was embedded in her memory forever was the one from the last day she spent in her old apartment with her mother. Hungry as always, Stefania was waiting from an early morning for her mother to come back home. But her mother didn't show up. Two days went by and finally, in the evening hours on the second day of Stefania's lonely hours, her mother appeared. She didn't carry any bag and she looked terrifying. Her clothes were ripped off, her nose was bleeding, her hair was in a mess, and she was barefoot. Her legs were in scars and the blood was all over her body. She collapsed to the floor of the living room and remained lying there motionless. Stefania waited half an hour and then tried to wake her up thinking that her mother had fallen asleep. But her mother didn't wake up. Stefania kept shaking her mother's body stubbornly hoping that eventually her mother would open her eyes and stand up. But it didn't happen. After an hour of unsuccessful trials to make her move, Stefania went outside and told a man who worked in a local shop that her mother didn't want to wake up. The man looked surprisingly at the little girl and then followed her back to the apartment. What he saw made shocked him. A dead woman covered in scars lay on the floor of the small apartment. After his phone call to someone, the police officers came and moved the motionless body. There were blood smears all around the floor where previously Stefania's mother had lain. And something that resembled the vomit, yellow and gross. When the police officers raised the body from the floor, Stefania for the last time looked at her mother's face. Her eyes were wide open. They were bulging and, for a moment, they caught a glimpse of the Stefania's static figure, and Stefania could swear she saw some terror in those eyes. As if her mother had seen or witnessed some frightening event. But Stefania would never find out what had happened to her mother, how she had got all those cuts and what had been the reason of her death.

After that, some nice people came, maybe the nicest people she had met up to then. They were social workers and they took her to the orphanage. The orphanage was a big and cold place, full of children, different ages, different physical features, different voices and different moods. Some of them were calm and confused. One could read fear in their eyes, and some distant sorrow that made them alien and not-belonging to any place. Others were aggressive and noisy. They were biting everything and everyone and they ruined anything they found. They couldn't accept the confines of the orphanage after years spent on the streets. And there was the third group of children. Those were the children who felt safe in this new place, felt relieved and sheltered, but still sad and lonely. They felt as if they had lost something or someone that had been their blood, their kin and everything they knew. But they didn't seem to miss that person. This new place brought some novelty that was in a certain way comfortable, but pretty cold and unemotional. They always felt cold, and they always needed an extra blanket to get their blood flow through their bodies. As if the cold walls of the orphanage had been made of ice and that ice had never melted. The cold eyes and the cold hands of the orphanage workers were not welcoming. They did everything that was expected from them to do: they served food to the children, gave them medications, gave them books and toys, but they didn't give them what those children needed the most: warmth, love, hugs and kisses. Stefania belonged to this last group.

And then, one sunny day, Mr. and Mrs. Kupinovski appeared. Dressed up as if they had been going to some official event with a lot of famous people, actors, politicians, bankers, brokers and musicians, they seemed overdressed for the place such was the orphanage where Stefania lived.

They walked hurriedly holding hands as school children and looking at each other happily. When they saw Stefania they almost ran toward her, as if they had recognized her from somewhere. It looked like they had seen her before. But it was impossible! Stefania had never seen these people.

She would have remembered their faces. They must have seen only her photo. That was how they had recognized her. They were accompanied by the social worker, the woman whose name was Tanya, and who took care of the children that shared the huge room with Stefania.

First, when Tanya had just met them, on the very entrance of the orphanage, Tanya seemed confused, unpleasantly. She spotted the euphoria that overcame Mr. and Mrs. Kupinovski when they noticed Stefania who was standing with Tanya in the corridor and waiting to meet her future parents for the first time. She didn't want them to scare her and she wanted some time to pass before they decide to adopt this little tortured, devastated, mournful, lonely little soul. Even though always stern, rarely smiling and laughing, Tanya was a good-hearted woman who cared about the orphans.

And she knew from the previous experience that those overenthusiastic couples often got very disappointed once they brought the adopted child home. Those couples, unable to have their own children, often created the image of the child they would like to have. That image was usually the perfection of a human being, quiet, cute, polite, kind, humble, with good manners and nice language. That image was more a doll or a robot programmed to do whatever the couple wanted and turn off whenever the new parents took off its batteries. They sometimes forgot that those orphans had been often malnourished, tortured, neglected, abandoned children with all kinds of traumas and phobias. They could not and they would probably never become the perfect examples of children.

They would always bear a trace of the twisted past that had deformed the part of their personality forever. Tanya seated Mr. and Mrs. Kupinovski and asked them to calm down. She reminded them that Stefania had had probably the troubled past, with a lot of difficult situations for a small child and that even though she seemed calm, she might be edgy and unsettled. She also told them that Stefania hadn't talked much about anything and she couldn't say if her talking would improve at any stage.

Mr. and Mrs. Kupinovski were ashamed of their behavior. They got back to their calm state and they tried to control their euphoria. They apologized for their hastiness and over-enthusiasm, but they blamed it on their desperate wish to have a child. They didn't care what kind of past and what kind of social misdemeanor the child had been involved in the past, they promised to make sure that that child was happy, healthy, and well-cared-for. They promised to provide anything necessary for Stefania's well-being and to approach all her problems and traumas together with the experts. Tanya seemed satisfied and admitted to herself that this couple looked and appeared reasonable enough to take care of the child with a knotty past that had removed the warmth from her eyes. And later, Mr. and Mrs. Kupinovski proved to be the good parents.

The family Kupinovski got another member, little Stefania. Martha and Tomas seemed pretty happy. Stefania blended well into her new environment, and didn't give much troubles to her new parents. She seemed to like them. Fiona helped her to start talking, not much though, but better anything than nothing.

Stefania was happy. Honestly happy. She had never had the coziness and warmth of a real home and no matter that nightmares often tortured her during the night, the morning light brought a relief. She never told anyone that in those nightmares, her real mother appeared with the cigarette in her hand ready to burn soft and hairless child's skin. But Stefania promised to herself to fight against those nightmares. She would overcome them without anyone's help. Alone, but not lonely.

The comfort of having parents gave her the strength to cope better with the secrets she kept and which she felt were safer if kept unknown. Even though Tanya had often told her that she would have felt better if she had talked to someone about everything that had bothered her, she knew that it was not the case with her. She felt better if she kept those dark events undisclosed. Eventually, their dismal features would fade away. Stefania believed in that. And she was happy and grateful that her parents let her be, let her keep her secrets, and never insisted on her revealing anything that she didn't want to. And Buskagrad as well. It let her do whatever she wanted without intruding into her privacy. Buskagrad made her feel safe and a little bit dumb but satisfied.

And she was right, slowly but surely, no matter how painful her past was, it started losing importance. Her current life was what mattered. Stefania's nightmares were rarely appearing as time passed by. She had less troubled thoughts and even the scars on her body seemed less visible. Her heart and soul appeared to be on a good way to be cured.

Maybe it was scientifically proven that talk helped people overcome difficult situations in their lives, but every rule had an exception. And Stefania's case was an exception. She was the deviation of the scientific rules, the anomaly in the human world, the tongue-tied oddity that refused to talk and still found a way through the silence to overcome the darkness of the past. She was a maverick among the ordinary people.

Speed Dating

The wailing of sirens. It didn't happen often in a small town as Berkville. Ambulance?

Maybe someone had a stroke, or even died. Police? Or someone made a false report of a bomb threat just to inject some excitement into the town's dullness.

Hanna was sitting in a chair and looking out the window. Such a beautiful day! Sunny, bright and warm. The winter cold had finally left the town. There were so many beautiful days in Berkville. Pity there were no more unusual events to make these days special.

Hanna had spent the entire life in Berkville. It was her whole universe and she didn't know any better. She knew there must have been some other amazing places out there to explore. But she was not an explorer, adventurer and vagabond. Her hometown lulled her into a strange sense of its uniqueness.

Hanna was a kind of a boring person. She didn't have many interests. When she had been a child, she had always played with the same doll. And she had always watched the same cartoon. She had known it by heart. Once she grew up, her personality remained the same. She stuck to the quality of singularity. She would always go to the same coffee shop and drink a hot cappuccino without sugar. She ate in the same restaurant once or twice per week. If she was very hungry, she ate a tuna steak with french fries. But if her hunger was not so intense, she ate a Greek salad with a lot of feta cheese.

Hanna had only one good friend, Susan, and they had known each other since kindergarten.

They shared everything they knew or found out and they knew absolutely everything about each other. Even when the last time one of them went to the dentist, had her period or migraine. Banalities they talked about every day were what actually entertained them. Anyway, there was not much to talk about.

Hanna and Susan worked in the same bank. Not in the same office, though. They ate lunch together and went home together every day. They lived in the same street. Same town, same bank, same street. They were doomed to sameness.

Hanna lived alone. Her parents had died few years ago, and her older brother had moved out from Berkville more than ten years ago. He was a journalist and he traveled a lot and he couldn't settle down to a small-town life. The last time Hanna had heard from him, a year ago, he had been in Myanmar.

Susan lived with her parents and grandma. They had a big house and Susan occupied the whole second floor.

Both Hanna and Susan were spinsters. They were in their mid-forties. For a small-town opinion, they were doomed and they would probably die alone. But it didn't seem to bother either Hanna or Susan.

Hanna was a tall blonde woman with a Roman nose, big blue eyes, high forehead, low brows and very thin lips, almost invisible. Her cheeks were a bit chubby but it only made her look younger. She had disproportional but quite unique features. She was not physically compelling but she was kind and well-mannered and no one could say anything bad about her.

Susan was brunette, pretty stout and short. Her chin-length bob made her face look even rounder. However, her hawk nose, charming almond-shaped green eyes and full lips gave her an exquisite beauty. She had always had a lot of admirers. Men buzzed around her not only because she was quite attractive but sharp-witted and energetic as well.

Hanna had always envied, a bit, her looks and inborn energy and enthusiasm, but not enough for one to say that she was jealous of Susan.

Hanna had never met a man who wanted to marry her. When she was twenty-two, she had dated an older man, who had been the same age of her father, for almost two years. However, he had made it clear that he hadn't wanted a wife and kids. He had been a divorcée and he enjoyed his freedom. Hanna had been a kind of his girlfriend, but that hadn't stopped him from occasionally seeing other women. Once Hanna had got fed up with all his womanizing fiestas, she had left him.

After him, she had had a few relationships, but nothing worth mentioning.

Susan, on the other hand, had always had men who had been deep in love with her. Almost all of her boyfriends had loved her and wanted to marry her. But she had never been ready for marriage and kids. When she had been thirty-five, she had fallen in love with a man her own age, who had also worked in the bank. They had dated for a year and then, he had proposed her. She had loved him and it had seemed to her that maybe she would be keen on marrying him. However, she had been scared. She had been afraid that the marriage would ruin her otherwise simple, content and easy life. She couldn't give up her own freedom. It had always been so precious to her. She had always lived in a self-contained bubble that opened up occasionally for other people, but just temporarily. Once they started feeling too comfortable in that bubble and occupied too much space of it, the bubble threw them out. And Susan had felt that she couldn't be free with a husband.

Therefore, she had said no to the man. The man had been brokenhearted. He had moved to the other town never to return. Susan had been sad after this event, and for many years, she hadn't dated any man.

The two friends, Hanna and Susan, appeared to be happy with a bit boring spinster lives.

Sometimes, they would express a desire to meet men with whom they would share their houses, beds and all other couple things. Hanna seemed to miss it more than Susan, but anyway, they were not desperate or depressed. They did what they wanted and they lived their own lives as they wished. Even though, for someone else, their lives were not something to envy, they were happy.

But something happened that shook their lives, as well as lives of many other Berkville citizens, mostly female.

A rich man, whose nickname, Goldie, everyone knew but almost no one knew his real name, and who was single as well, and who was famous in entertainment industry, opened The Speed Date Rooftop Garden. This totally new, and up to then, unusual place, was on the top of the tallest building in Berkville, on its seventh floor. The whole town could be seen from there and nights filled with start and moonlight were a beautiful spectacle.

There were no similar places miles and miles around. There were no speed date centers or similar dating clubs even in other towns nearby. The novelty of the whole idea brought Goldie a lot of success. The Speed Date Rooftop Garden attracted a lot of people. Those people were of all ages, professions, and interests. There were bachelors, spinsters, divorcées, widows and widowers. There were teachers, bankers, economists, engineers, writers, accountants, waitresses, masseurs, gardeners, designers, miners, brokers, firemen, chefs, cooks.

The Speed Date Rooftop Garden was open twice per week, on Friday and Saturday, from seven in the evening until midnight. And it worked like this: during the first two hours, from seven until nine, following ten minutes of conversation, a bell was rung, and all gathered men proceeded to the next lady, and then another ten-minute conversation began. The ladies always remained seated at their own tables. After each speed date, both men and women marked on their cards if they were interested in meeting their date again. These cards carried all the likes and dislikes of the place. They were disappointment initiator and match maker. These card were at nine o'clock delivered to the hosts who would later on, probably after midnight or the very next morning, provide those who had showed a mutual interest in seeing each other again with the other person's contact information. From nine until midnight, the band was playing and food and drinks were served. People usually mingled.

Hanna and Susan attended these speed date events. Susan had always had more matches, but after the first real date with any of her matches, she would decide not to see her match again. Even though, there were many interesting men she had met during those speed date nights, they seemed less interesting when on a real date with her.

Hanna's first real dates were partially successful. There was a banker she was seeing for sometime after their real date. But it turned out that he still hadn't forgotten his ex-wife and was not ready to move on and date someone else. Hanna was disappointed but not so much. She liked the banker but not enough to fall in love with him. Disappointments seemed to become so normal and casual that she didn't make a big deal of them. She would meet them, greet them, and let them go. That's how she dealt with disappointments.

One Friday night, after a month of skipping speed date events, both Hanna and Susan decided to visit The Speed Date Rooftop Garden and try their luck.

As usual, The Speed Date Rooftop Garden was full of people. For two hours, all of them were speed dating, nervously smiling, asking questions, giving awkward or already rehearsed answers, and more or less, enjoying the evening.

After the speed dates, Hanna and Susan sat together and chatted looking around and making some cheeky comments. They both noticed that that night they both had had the speed date with a handsome accountant who obviously had charmed both of them. His name was Frank and he used to live in a big city. However, Frank planned to move to Berkville in a month since he had inherited a house from his grandfather who had just passed away. He was tired of the city life and wanted to settle down, have family and lead a quiet life. Frank was a perfect catch for small-town girls.

The very next morning, Hanna and Susan learned that Frank had showed interest in both of them.

They hurried to tell each other the news and then after, they giggled like school girls. But for the first time, they both decided not to tell each other what they planned to wear for the date with Frank, what they intended to ask him and what secret weapon they would use to seduce him. These things remained secret. Despite the fact that they knew each other so well and that they probably suspected what the other one was planning, they decided not to talk about it.

Hanna was not as self-confident as Susan, and she feared that after the first real date, Frank might and probably would decide to continue seeing Susan. She felt sadness overcome her but she tried to keep calm.

Susan was quite confident that she would win this man. She believed that Hanna didn't have much chance with Frank. Even though she loved her friend, she thought that Frank was out of Hanna's league. She was too reserved, clumsy, insecure, meek. Frank seemed like a man who wanted a different type of a woman. Someone who would not be submissive but equal, someone who had the same energy as he did and someone who looked him in the eye when they talked. And that woman was Susan.

Both Hanna and Susan seemed happy with the outcome of their first real date with Frank.

Hanna believed that his smile, questions he had kept asking her, gentle touch of her hand and the way he had flattered her a little bit, meant that they would keep seeing each other. At the end of the evening, he even kissed her cheek gently, held her hand for a while and promised to call her the next day. Hanna had butterflies in her stomach.

Susan was certain that their first real date was a complete success. He laughed loudly at her jokes. And he smiled every time she started talking. He looked her in the eyes and many times during the evening mentioned that he had never seen such beautiful eyes. He walked her back home, since it was not far from the restaurant where they had had dinner, and promised to call her the following day.

Hanna and Susan didn't call each other to tell how the date with Frank had been. They kept that for themselves and waited the following day and Frank's call.

The next day, both of them were nervous, roaming around the living room and place where the telephone was. Hanna picked up the receiver twice to check if the phone was working, and Susan smoked cigarette by cigarette nervously waiting for the damn phone to ring.

The phone never rang either in Hanna's living room or in Susan's corridor. They didn't hear from Frank that or the next day.

On Monday morning, they didn't talk too much to each other at work and neither of them mentioned Frank. As if they had silently agreed that Frank was a forbidden topic. And they also felt that neither of them was lucky. They felt sorry for each other, but kept distance since it was awkward for both of them to talk now when they were hurt and disappointed. Hanna, who had faced so many disappointments, handled another one pretty well, but Susan, the constant winner, was not capable of sorting out how and why this disappointment had struck her. She was overemotional at home, frustrated at work and on the verge of tears all the time.

A week passed and Hanna and Susan still didn't spend so much together. But they slowly started forgetting the failed episode with Frank.

Then, there were rumors in the bank that a handsome accountant who had been seen around lately, had started dating a local rich widow Joanna. Joanna was a rich woman in her mid-fifties whose husband had died three years ago and he had left her all the wealth he had gained for many years working as an art dealer. Joanna was financially secure for life. She had been probably a pretty woman once, and she still had a pleasant face, but in her fifties, she was overweight and not attractive. Normally, the guys like Frank did not pay attention to the women like Joanna. But this Frank was an exemption.

The small and boring town of Berkville got the entertainment. The speculations and gossips about Joanna and Frank were the prime time news. The rich woman and the handsome man couldn't escape discerning eyes of Berkville citizens. They were surprised but the wealth of the widow Joanna would have attracted not only Frank but many other men. Anyway, they didn't know something about Frank that sooner rather than later would bring a shocking dose of interest among people in Berkville.

When Hanna and Susan heard those gossips about Frank and Joanna, they somehow forgot their own failure to seduce this man. The curiosity of the whole affair brought them back to each other. Finally, they talked about Frank and their disappointment and focused on repeating the gossips they had heard.

Frank and Joanna rarely appeared in public together. Once in a while, someone would see them eating in some of the most expensive restaurants in town, or they would visit the golf club.

While Frank was playing golf, Joanna would sit in the VIP seat far from the hungry-for-gossip eyes of people and usually read a book and drink a cocktail.

No more than two months passed and someone heard from the local municipal clerk that Joanna and Frank got married. They got married with just two witnesses and Joanna's daughter who had come from the capital to attend this simple ceremony. There was no party, no celebration and no invitees from Berkville. The whole thing aroused even more curiosity. People in Berkville were intrigued by the simplicity of the wedding process. Rich people usually loved showing off. But something here was fishy.

And not that long after, someone who had known Frank's grandpa and the financial situation of the Frank's family told someone else in secret and that one again confided to someone else that Frank had inherited not only the grandpa's house but his huge debts as well. Poor Frank had had no much choice. He had had to abandon his pretty nonchalant lifestyle and come to this tedious town to take care of debts. And he had seemed to have found an easier way to do this task. He had decided to find a rich wife. And he had succeeded. He had found the goose that laid the golden eggs.

When Hanna and Susan heard this, they breathed a sigh of relief. They thanked dear God Frank hadn't chosen one of them! Anyway, they were not wealthy enough for him. They both reminisced about their dates with Frank and how he had been curious about their salaries, finances, inheritance. They hadn't paid attention to those questions before. But suddenly, everything seemed clear!

The hot news was repeated and retold in many different versions for some weeks, maybe a month, and then the news became just warm and finally cooled off. Once in a while, someone would notice that Frank was rarely in Berkville and that he had been often seen in the capital's famous clubs. Some wicked tongues spread rumors that Frank didn't even sleep anymore with his wife, while the others claimed that he had been seen with other women.

Slowly but surely, Hanna and Susan forgot about the failed dates with Frank. They went back to their normal life, but not the one before the Speed Date Rooftop Garden. That life had been totally forgotten. They went back to the one after. They visited this place often. Once in a while, they met some interesting men and dated them for some time. And they continued to work in the same bank, eat their lunch together and share with each other everything. Every now and then, they would hear that Frank had beaten up his wife, and that she had stopped going out, and that he had forbidden her daughter to come back home. But the news was not the breaking news anymore. The drowning of a child in the town's lake, a new presidential election, and the cheating scandal of the famous actress somehow put everything else in the shade. The world was moving. So did Berkville, even though in slow motion.

Onion Tears

Lola cried a river that day. Once her tears burst out, she couldn't stop them. They kept running down her face like the water that escaped its usual boundaries during the flood. The tears also escaped the confines of her body. And they ran freely. They were unstoppable. The reason, or at least the main reason, the one that was to blame for this flood was the one not habitually occurring. Lola didn't start crying because she was sad or happy. Sadness and happiness had nothing to do with her crying. At least not initially and ostensibly. She cried because she was cutting onions.

She started cutting onions in order to prepare dinner. What seemed a simple house chore turned into uncontrollable weeping, the release of the stinging tears of frustration. Probably piled frustration. And what she noticed was that the stinging was not unpleasant at all. Quite the opposite. The shedding of tears brought her some comfort and solace as if she had just released the burden that had imprisoned her for so long. She had been held captive by distress, heartache, pain. And just the simple act of cutting onions caused those tormenting emotions to become bearable.

Few months ago, Lola's mother died. Lola's mother, Mrs. Kupinski, was Lola's only real friend. She was her mother but the mother's figure was superseded by the fact that she behaved as if she had been Lola's friend. They went to the cinema together, had a couple of drinks in the city's bars, flirted with men, gossiped, traveled and fought over unimportant issues.

Mrs. Kupinski's authority over Lola was diminished by the fact that she had never had parents. At least she had never met them. She was an orphan, never adopted and never taken care of. When she was big enough and had to leave the orphanage, to experience the life upheaval or its downfall, to find her own way and create her own home, she was on her own. Completely alone and absolutely bewildered. Fear and confusion led her to the man who neither loved her not wanted her children.

He was a member of high society, a broker with social status whose ancestors had been well-known and wealthy. His name was Ted. Ted enjoyed flirting with women and he indulged in casual sex, and when he met Mrs. Kupinski, her naivety, innocence and extraordinary beauty impressed him.

He told himself that he had to have her, to possess her for some time until he got bored of her. And he seduced her. He was an excellent in winning over women, enticing them, deliberately tricking them and luring them into the trap of false and unrequited love. Once, he lost the interest for Mrs.

Kupinski, Ted cast her away together with their unborn baby. And he threatened her that he would hurt her if she revealed that the baby was his. His cruelty had no measures. He was brutal in his ignorance of other people's feelings and needs.

Mrs. Kupinski, alone, abandoned, rejected and miserable, first felt into the depression hole that seemed like the deep abyss. The dark bottomless pit from which she thought she could never escape. But the baby that was growing in her stomach made her collect her strength and will-power that had still remained in her broken body and soul. She found a job in the local telecommunications company and decided to do everything that was in her power to bring the healthy baby to this world. She ate regularly, avoided conflicts and arguments, slept enough and walked a couple of hours every day. All on her own. The feeling so familiar. But not for long. She looked forward to the day when her baby would be born. And somehow, led by her mother's instinct, she knew that it would be a girl. And she was right.

Lola was born on a sunny April morning. The birds were chirping, sun rays wriggled through the air and spring colors which were reflected in the abundance of flowers everywhere welcomed the baby girl to the world. Another miracle in this world. Mrs. Kupninski couldn't have been happier. She shed tears of joy and forgot all the misery she had faced in her life. From that day, the new life for her began. The life of shared happiness, smiles, hugs, cuddles, kisses. The life of mother-hood and real friendship. Lola transformed her life into a fairy tale.

When Lola thought about those days she had spent with her mother, she realized that her mother had been everything to her and she had always been there for Lola. They had been rarely separated and it had been only for a day or two. And everything Lola knew, she had learned from her mother. Schools gave her some interesting theoretical mostly knowledge, but her mother was her best and favorite teacher. She thought her many life lessons. How was she supposed to live without her?

Lola didn't have many friends. Isolated in her own world that consisted entirely of her mother and her, she hadn't learned how to make friendships. If someone offered her a hand of friendship, she accepted it, but she had never made the initiative to find and make new friends. She seemed to be an overprotected child. Her mother also made sure to be whatever Lola needed her to be. Therefore, Lola was deprived of the need and skills to make friends. Actually, she knew only two people she could call the friends.

An older lady, her first neighbor, Mrs. Stanislavski, who lived alone in a small apartment next to the Lola's place. She loved baking and often brought vanilla cookies, cinnamon rolls, raisin strudel, ginger and banana bread to Lola. She also didn't have anyone. Her husband had passed away ten years ago, as well as her two older sisters. Mrs. Stanislavski didn't have children. And her only hobbies were baking, reading and feeding the pigeons who regularly came to her balcony and cooed gently asking for her attention and food.

The other friend or better the acquaintance was Alex. She was not sure if he was her friend because they had known each other only for six months, since he had started working as a sous chef in the restaurant called Onion. She and her mother had loved Onion and visited it regularly. After her mother had passed away, Lola went there only twice. Avoidance of everything familiar that she had shared with her mother was the safest way not to deal with the pain. She was just postponing the flood of tears that eventually had to come out.

The first time when Alex accidentally met her on the street and asked her why she and he mother hadn't been in Onion for a long time, Lola went numb and out of tune with herself. She forgot that they were walking along the pavement and she just let herself sit down on the curb as if she had lost all the strength and felt she couldn't walk anymore. Her emotional numbness followed.

She told him that her mother had passed away and her tearless face showed that she was still shocked and stunned by the loss of her mother. Alex was sad that he asked her this but he didn't know anything about the death of Mrs. Kupinski. He helped her stand up and persuaded her to come and try his dish of the day, grilled Teriyaki tuna. Even though Lola didn't have much appetite during those days and skipped regularly meals or just forgot to eat, she couldn't refuse his kind invitation.

Alex was persuasive. He promised her she would be happier after the meal and it would be probably the best Teriyaki tuna she had ever tried. And it was! Plus, Alex made a delicious blueberry cheesecake especially for Lola. Somehow, he remembered that Lola had a sweet tooth. That day was probably one of the best days after her mother had died. At the end of the afternoon, when she finished the last bites of her blueberry cheesecake and got ready to leave, Alex appeared from the restaurant's kitchen with a box full of different cakes that were real delicacies. He gave it to her, wished her good evening and asked her to come back soon. He promised to make for her something special. She smiled. She forgot when she had smiled the last time. That was something new. She was maybe opening the door to a new skill, the skill to make friends. That possibility gave her pleasure. She also caught his glance that looked for her eyes. He seemed eager to tell her that everything would be all right, just he didn't say it. But she read it on his face. The words were unnecessary. His discerning eyes were easy to read. Or at least it seemed like that to her. No other man showed such an attitude and care for her loss. For a moment, she felt as if she had been a pop star, a beautiful singer or maybe a famous actress who attracted men's attention and admiration. Of course, she dreamed awake. Nothing wrong with that. She felt shy at the same time. Maybe she just exaggerated everything, and misread his gestures. But he was very kind and she believed that was how friends behaved. Lola bowed her head willing to hide her blushing and rosy cheeks, smiled again, said "goodbye" and left.

The second time, she initiated the meeting. That was the second step in learning new skills. The initiative. Or just the response to Alex's invitation to come back soon to the restaurant. She went to Onion at midday to have lunch, a little bit earlier than everyone else usually had lunch. She knew that if she avoided the rush lunch hour, she might be able to see Alex and maybe he would be free to sit and chat with her a bit. She needed a good company and she couldn't think of anyone better than Alex. She entered the restaurant cautiously as if she had entered some sacred place. She wanted to be noticed and to call for Alex's attention but at the same time, she didn't want to disturb the serene atmosphere this place breathed in that day. There was only one couple having their meal at the very far corner of Onion. She sat somewhere in the middle of the restaurant, the place that was visible from all sides, and she made sure to say loudly "hello" to the waiters and barman. Lola didn't have any secret weapon prepared to bring Alex out of the kitchen, and she hoped that he would show up accidentally and talk to her at least for a while. He turned out to be her mood booster. She ordered a simple mixed salad and a glass of white wine. Alex didn't show up the first half an hour but she heard his voice coming from the kitchen. When she got her salad and wine, he came out and joined her at the table. He didn't expect to see her and was pleasantly surprised. He was smiling and it was a genuinely kind smile. That smile made her feel better. She thanked him silently for that, not letting him know what she thought. But she suspected he knew. Somehow it seemed to her that their actions, thoughts, smiles, talks beat in the same rhythm. And she even thought that he was doing everything in his power to make her feel better.

That made her like him more. It was natural and unforced. Liking him was so effortless. They spent half an hour chatting and when the crowd started filling the restaurant, Lola decided to leave. She felt a thousand times better than she had felt before she had come to Onion.

And now she was standing and crying over the onions she had cut. There were so many of them. In the fridge as well. She could fill few big pots with those cut pieces. Maybe even more.

When she had started cutting onions, there had been only two big onions she had intended to cut.

But then she realized how therapeutic this act was and she went to the shop and bought two kilos more. While cutting them she was not fully aware of the fact that she would have too many onion cuts. She was so focused on her memories and stress-relieving tears and the pain that she started letting out of her agonized body and soul. And once she finished cutting the last onion and wanted to continue with this pain-alleviating action, she came to her senses. It was enough for today! And it was helpful! Thank you dear onions!

But what would she do with all those onions cuts? If she put them in the fridge or freezer, and didn't eat them soon, they would get spoiled and she would have to throw them away. And she was repelled by the thought of throwing food. Out of the blue, it came to her! The restaurants always needed a lot of fresh-cut vegetables, and they would use it the very same day! Therefore, she decided to take the onion cuts to Onion and give them to Alex. They helped her and they would definitely help Alex to make some delicious dishes that day. She smiled at the thought of it.

After she took a shower, dressed and put all those onion cuts in the big plastic bags, she went outside and walked to Onion. The smell of onion spread behind her and people, the random passersby, turned around and looked at her surprised that such a beautiful girl had chosen such a terrible perfume. She laughed to herself as she thought about it. When she entered Onion, she wished the waiters good evening and asked if Alex was around. One of the waiters went into the kitchen to call Alex. Alex appeared after a minute a bit surprised to see her but very happy. When he saw the plastic bags she held and felt the strong smell of onion, he smiled a bit confused. She approached him and told him honestly that she had cut too many onions and that she didn't know what to do with them. She thought Alex would be able to use them. Her red swollen and beautiful eyes revealed the secret, the reason why she had cut so many onions. At least it was clear to him.

Others probably couldn't understand and they thought that she had been silly or she had been supposed to prepare a big dinner for a lot of people, but in the end, dinner had been canceled.

Alex smiled politely and thanked her. He made a joke that they could feed the whole town tonight with all the onion cuts she had made. Lola was in a good mood thanks to the onions. And Alex was grateful to them as well. He invited Lola to stay and have dinner in Onion and since she had nothing else to do she accepted. There were no many people in the restaurant that night and Alex could have a break and have dinner with Lola. He prepared Lamb and onion curry and while they devoured the delicious dish full of onion, they both smiled and joked that probably people would avoid them that evening and probably the next day because of the robust onion smell they gave off. Alex said that maybe they should stick together and avoid other people while the smell disappeared and Lola smiled showing that she liked the idea.

That evening they talked a lot and after Alex finished his work, he walked Lola home, He kissed her cheek gently and asked her if she was willing to join him for breakfast next morning in the beautiful café on the river bank. Lola was not able to refuse anything Alex suggested. She said "yes", gave him another onion kiss on the cheek and went to her apartment to dream some pleasant dreams filled with onion smell.

Brain Crack

The street was my home. I spent half of my life on the street. And I had no other home for a long time. There must have been better and more comfortable ones, but that one was mine. Therefore, it was good enough. I didn't know for better.

I was only thirteen when I started roaming the streets and rummaging for food. I had never met my parents. They told me I had never had ones. But there must have been a man and a woman who had made me. What had happened to them I didn't know and I didn't think I would even find out.

I spent thirteen years in an orphanage, that filthy hole. The orphanage employees were not kind and friendly, and led by their example, the orphans were also cruel, rude, moody and gruesome. The orphanage employees were not very creative with naming the orphans. They have me the name John. What a boring name! Or who knew, maybe someone else named me.

I hated that place. And finally, when I was thirteen, I ran away. I didn't think anyone there missed me. And they obviously didn't put much effort to catch me and bring me back.

First, I starved for days. I didn't know where to look for food, how to steal and what to do. My inexperience cost me an empty stomach. No one would give a job to a 13-year-old orphan either.

And there was not much I could do.

But then, I met an old man, Vilo. He was also roaming the streets. Bu he did that voluntarily. When His wife died, he left his house with only his clothes on, and never went back. He told me he had wanted to die at the beginning. But the power of will to live won. He felt hungry and he searched for food. In the garbage bins, restaurants garbage containers, wherever he thought he could find some scraps and leftovers. It was not the life he had to live. He had a good pension and a nice house. But he chose the street life.

I had always thought that something must have cracked in his head. And that crack, that hole, the cavity which was empty and void needed to be filled. Otherwise, his brain couldn't function normally. The death of his wife made that hole, and his old life couldn't fill it. Therefore, he opted for the street life.

I had never lost anything that I had had in that time, because I had never had anything. And I believed that instead of a brain, my skull was filled with the void. That nothingness couldn't be easily filled since it preserved empty for so long. And I didn't know what could be a good filler, until I met Vilo.

When Vilo was in a good mood, which means his crack was calm, and it didn't happen often, he told me about his wife and children. He had two sons who were married and had their own families.

All of them were trying hard to bring Vilo to his senses. They often came to the area where Vilo slept and hung out, brought him food and clothes and tried to talk to him. Sometimes, he accepted the food, clothes and kind words and he listened to his sons and grandchildren, but often, he refused everything they offered him and ran away.

I looked at those clean, good-looking and pleasant people and thought how happy I would be to have my own family.

That would be my brain filler. I wished not only to have the house but home, household, people that would fill those empty rooms and bring liveliness to otherwise just a building. But how to make this dream come true?

One day, the older Vilo's son, Joyce, came to see his father. Vilo and I were sitting on the cardboard sheets in front of an abandoned building. When Vilo saw his son, he picked up his scraps and ran away. I remained to at least try to comfort Joyce, since he seemed sad and disappointed that his own father didn't want to see him. Even though he must have already got used to Vilo's strange behavior, Joyce always seemed broken-hearted when Vilo refused his gifts and company. I felt sorry for Joyce.

Joyce sat down on one of the cardboard sheets and started telling me how he had had a hard day at work and that he had hoped his father would at least be in a good mood and make him feel better.

Being a carpenter was a nice thing and he loved his job except when your bosses got nasty and started complaining about everything you did. I wondered what the carpenter's day looked like.

Seeing my curiosity, Joyce face lightened. He looked in my eyes and told me that if I really wanted to see how the carpenter spent his working day, I could join him the next day at work and watch him working.

I was pretty excited about Joyce's offer. But I looked at my ragged clothes that were also very dirty and got ashamed. Joyce understood my hesitation to accept his offer and he told me he would give me some clothes and that I could even take shower in the shower room of his company. I smiled and looked forward to the next day.

Becoming a carpenter was not easy. But at the same time, it was not that difficult either. And I wanted to learn carpentry skill. Joyce was happy. He promised to teach me and train me. In exchange, I would help him out when necessary, when he alone was not able to finish a job on the scheduled time. Of course, I would get paid for it.

The excitement of learning made me a great student. My curiosity and motivation impressed Joyce.

And he was a patient teacher. No reprimands came from him. He always made sure to explain me, with a caring voice what I did wrong. In a month, I was able to do some tasks he gave me alone.

In the meantime, Vilo continued his roaming the streets aimlessly and carelessly. Once I felt the comfort of working and earning money, I started struggling to understand why this old man had abandoned all the benefits of the normal life. I knew that the hole in his brain was different than mine, but I didn't know how to persuade him to come back to his old life. He just didn't want the old life. He wanted something new, different from the painful memory.

Well, I wanted the same: something new but better.

After few months of working as the carpenter with Joyce, I earned enough money to rent a small room and buy some clothes. Joyce was, however, very generous and he gave me a lot of his clothing pieces that he hadn't worn anymore. I was eternally grateful for everything he had done for me.

Months went by and I was doing fine working and living the life I loved. It seemed to me that I had been just born and that I was just getting to know the beauty of living.

Then, I met Maria, a girl who worked as a cashier in the local store and we started dating. Maria was a short, almond-eyed brunette whose smile bought me the first time I saw her. For the first time in my life, I felt truly loved and wanted. I realized that there was no bigger award in life than to share happiness with the people you loved. And I was awarded: I was happy, loved and I loved someone deeply and honestly.

Maria and I got married after six months of dating. We managed to buy a small apartment on the outskirts of the town. Those were the best days of my life.

When Maria stayed pregnant, my happiness was lifted to exhilaration. I was so excited that I would become a father and that there would be another small human being on this planet thanks to Maria and me that I told everyone the news: friends, Joyce, acquaintances, passersby. They all seemed happy for me even those who saw me for the first time.

During the eighth month of pregnancy, as her belly was growing, her anxiety and some strange pain in the abdomen grew as well. She started feeling unwell very often. Dizziness, weakness, pain, migraines tortured her and she was hospitalized.

My blood ran cold those days. I feared the worst. And unfortunately, the worst thing one could imagine happened to me. I lost Maria and our baby. The miscarriage ended up with Maria's death as well. And her death opened another huge hole not only in my brain but in my heart also. The pain I felt was unbearable. And those holes inflicted agony I didn't know how to fight against. And I didn't fight. I just let it be.

The next few weeks, I was a dead man walking. Actually, I didn't even walk, I didn't go outside. I stayed inside the dark apartment with the curtains pulled down day and night. The stale air was suffocating but I didn't care. I couldn't eat, I couldn't move, I couldn't think or work. It seemed as if my whole world had fallen apart. And I wondered what I was doing alive here anyway.

Joyce kept calling me and stopping by my place and he tried to help but I didn't want any help.

Then, one day, not sure if it was morning, afternoon or evening, someone knocked on my door. I knew it was not

Joyce, because he would enter my apartment without my response to his knocking or ringing the bell. He would bring me the food, try to make some order in my small and messy room and then leave. But this knocking was different and persistent. It lasted almost fifteen minutes.

And it had intention to bring me up from my bed and make me move. It succeeded.

I reluctantly stood up and dragged myself to the door. When I opened the door, and unexpected surprise greeted me. Vilo was standing there in his rags. Strong but familiar odor was spreading around him. That odor reminded me of the years spent on the street. And I didn't miss it. But now, after being left alone, emotionally smashed and dispirited, I started thinking about the street life.

Vilo looked at me with his big blue watery eyes and said he was sorry for my loss. He seemed in a good mood. I gestured him to come in. He unwillingly obeyed but refused to sit on the sofa or in a chair since he didn't want to make them dirty. Instead, he just spread some old newspaper sheets on the floor and sat there. I felt embarrassed. I was so ashamed that he had done this for me and I felt so uncomfortable that I sat with him on the floor.

After a couple of minutes of complete silence, he asked me what I intended to do. I looked at him surprised by the question and asked: "To do with what?"

"To do with your life, son." He said calmly.

That was not the question I expected from him. He caught me completely off guard. I didn't know what to answer. And I remained silent.

Then he said: "I know you are thinking of leaving all of this: everything that you have achieved and made, everything that you have dreamed of. I know that you just want all that to go to hell and you don't want to know about it anymore. That life brings the memory of those who were gone. And that wound is so fresh that it seems impossible to heal. I know that you just want to get drunk, wasted, high. You just want to forget, actually, not to think about it. I know that. You want to run away from what hurts you. And that pain seems unbearable. I know that because I've been there.

And you even think about going back to the street, about joining me in this endless drifting and roaming life. I can feel it. I can read your thoughts. Well, I don't blame you for your thoughts. I understand them, but I don't support them.

Listen to me, young man. You probably now look at me and think: what is this old fool saying?! Is He mad?!Yes, I am. And that is the reason why I chose this kind of life. You know me well, and you know that I have that crack in my head. And when that crack gets nervous, I change completely.

Some kind of strange madness possesses me. I cannot control what I am doing and I don't recognize people, places and I don't know what I am capable of making. Maybe I can hurt someone, kill someone, make some irreparable damage. I don't know, because in those situations, I don't have control over my actions. That is the reason why I left my house, my children and grandchildren. I don't want to hurt them in those kind of spaced-out moments. I don't want to harm them. I would never forgive myself. However, I don't want to be locked in some asylum, prison or some other spooky institution either, where they would drug me and keep me locked and shackled. I prefer this kind of freedom than that kind of prison.

But you are different. Yes, you have some crack in your brain as well, but that crack, that hole is not like mine. You are young, strong and you can control your emotions. You can and you should rise above the misery and pain you have involuntarily embraced. You can pick up strength and continue doing what you love. There is the whole world out there you need to discover. It is waiting for you.

You can't go back to something you ran away from."

Then, he stopped talking. I saw that his eyes became different, not focused and a bit blurred. He started fidgeting and he became restless. He wanted to do something but he didn't know what. The crack in his brain took over control. Unexpectedly and all of a sudden.

At once, he just stood up and left.

I remained sitting on the floor for a long time. I was baffled. This Vilo was a man that I had just met. The old Vilo and I never talked about this kind of matters. The old Vilo was a senile man who didn't talk much. But he was good company. The new Vilo left me speechless. But he did provoke some emotions in me. For the first time, I felt that I had talked to someone who had authority to influence my feelings, to someone who was the father figure and had that strange power to make me do what he had asked me to. I was a child again.

When finally, I woke up from this bewilderment, from a trance that caused my cracked brain work again, I stood up, looked around the room and realized how messy and dirty it was. I opened the windows, let the air and sunlight in and started cleaning my home.

Strange behavior Tanya was playing in the garden while her grandpa and his friend Uncle Filip were discussing some serious grown-up matters.

Tanya was seven and she loved her grandparents' garden. There were plenty of flowers, herbs, trees, fruits. It was an oasis in the center of her hometown, hidden between tall buildings and the town's library. Whenever she visited her grandparents, she spent hours with them or alone in the garden.

That day, she carried a basket in which she put the rasp-berries that she picked up and ran after the colorful butterflies admiring the mosaic-like patterns on their small bodies. She laughed and talked to flowers and didn't even notice that her grandpa had left the garden and that Uncle Filip watched her playing. His discerning eyes woke her up from her reverie and interrupted her game and she noticed his strange goatee, white hair and wrinkled forehead. He approached her and asked her what game she was playing. She told him that her game didn't have any name but she started describing it. Involved into talking about what and how she was playing, she didn't no-tice that Uncle Filip came even closer and that his tall figure was standing next to her tiny one. Out of blue, he grabbed her head and pulled firmly her body against his while he was bending down. And he pressed his wet cigarette-tasting lips to her mouth.

The disgusting smell of his breath and his saliva leaving the trace on her lips petrified her. She was shocked and numbed but soon enough, she kicked and fought escaping his grip. She pushed Uncle Filip as strongly as she could, leaving her basket full of raspberries behind and ran to the house.

There was no one there, at least not in the living room. She entered her grandma's toilet and locked herself inside. Her body was shaking and her lips trembled due to some unusual fear and disgust.

What was it? Why did Uncle Filip kiss her that way? Kids were not supposed to be kissed by grown-ups like that.

She washed her face and sat on the floor of the toilet not sure what to do. She was afraid of Uncle Filip. She didn't want him to touch her again. She didn't want to see him.

Tanya was not sure how long she was in the toilet but when after some time she heard the footsteps outside approaching the toilet door, her heart started beating fast and she almost screamed in fear and panic.

Was it Uncle Filip looking for her? Was he going to break the door?

She closed her eyes and prayed. She prayed never again to see Uncle Filip. Tears started running down her face when the gentle voice of her grandpa spread through the air. He was looking for her.

"Tanya? Are you in the toilet, sweetheart? Uncle Filip told me you saw the snake in the garden and you ran away. Everything is ok, honey. I looked around and I didn't find it. It must have got scared as well and ran away. Don't worry. Those snakes that you sometimes see in our garden are harmless to people."

Tanya felt relieved. She was so happy to hear her grandpa's voice that she didn't remember if she had been ever happier in her whole life. Her grandpa was her savior. But she couldn't understand why Uncle Filip had made up the story about the snake. Did he intend to hurt Tanya?

Did he want to do something else to her, something bad and harmful? Should she tell her grandpa about what had happened in the garden? Would he believe her? Uncle Filip was his friend. And he had already told him the lie about the snake. Her grandpa believed him. Maybe he would not believe her story.

Tanya unlocked the toilet door and jumped into her grandpa's arms, warm tears running down her cheeks. She was so happy to see her grandpa. She didn't tell him anything about the strange behavior of Uncle Filip. She decided to keep silent. Anyway, she didn't understand why Uncle Filip had behaved like that and if it was acceptable or not. She only knew that she was disgusted by his strange behavior.

From that day, Tanya avoided Uncle Filip. If she knew he was in her grandparents' house, she didn't want to visit them.

If she accidentally saw him from afar, she turned around and prevented coming across him. She avoided the very sight of him. She was afraid and scared even of his shadow.

And she was lucky. She didn't meet him that often.

Years went by, and Tanya slowly pushed the memory of Uncle Filip and his strange behavior out of her mind. Once in a while, she would remember the unpleasant scene but as the time passed, it happened less frequently.

She enrolled the University of Social Sciences in the capital. She moved there and committed herself to studies that she quite enjoyed. Every six months, she would go back home to visit her family and spend some time with dear people.

One summer, when the university let its students enjoy summer holidays, Tanya went back to her hometown. After six months of not being at home, the homesickness grew in her and she was happier than ever to spend summer at home. It was hot summer and she spent it swimming in the river, reading, seeing her childhood friends, visiting her grandparents and enjoying every single moment.

One afternoon, after reading for few hours, she decided to stretch her legs and walk around the town. The road took her to the town's park and she sat on the bench and watched the children playing in the sand of the playground. She remembered her own happy childhood days. There were few parents sitting on the benches, a stray dog strolling around and an old man with a cane sitting on the bench close to the playground and watching the children playing. First, Tanya didn't pay special attention to anyone in particular. She enjoyed the warm air, bird song and children's playing.

But her attention got caught by the old man's unusual staring at children. She focused on him.

There was something uncommon and deviant in the way his eyes devoured children. The memory that she had left aside and almost forgot struck her and she recognized the goatee, wrinkled face, white hair. Even though much older now, it was the odd face of Uncle Filip. Tanya's heart started beating fast and the blood rushed to her head. She felt like a seven-year-old girl who had run away from the garden and locked herself in her grandparents' toilet. But this time, she knew that what Uncle Filip had done and was doing now was not right, and not acceptable.

Even though furious and incensed, she tried to calm herself and remained sitting on the bench looking at Uncle Filip. For more than half an hour he sat on the bench examining the children's play like some ordinary old man who reminisced his own childhood days. Most of the children, after some time, went home or were dragged by the parents who interrupted their playing, except two little blonde girls.

They remained in the playground. Both of them kept climbing the top of the slide via the ladder, sat down on the top of the slide and slid down the chute. They repeated it again and again.

Uncle Filip stood up, came closer to the slide and started talking to the little girls. Their attention was directed toward him for few minutes but then they continued their game. Uncle Filip remained standing in the same place. After a while, he took something from his pocket and extended his hand toward little girls holding that something that he had just fetched out. Tanya thought those were probably candies. The little girls finally stopped sliding and came closer to Uncle Filip. They took the candies, unwrapped them and started eating them. Burst of rage activated Tanya. She jumped to her feet and almost ran toward the old man and little girls. Once she came few meters from them, she realized she was right. Uncle Filip gave the candies to the girls and talked to them grinning slyly. Tanya couldn't bear the whole situation afraid what might happen next. She was repulsed by the thought that Uncle Filip intended to do something awfully inappropriate. And she decided to stop it, immediately and irrevocably.

"Hi girls, is this your grandpa," she addressed the little girls completely ignoring Uncle Filip. The children shook their heads no. "Then you should not talk to him or take anything he offers you. I am sure your parents already told you not to talk to strangers and take anything from them. It can be dangerous. You can't know if those strangers are good or bad people and if they want to hurt your or not. And some of them have bad intentions." After saying this, she turned around slightly and glanced at the old man who remained standing in the same spot without even changing his face expression. She was sure he had heard what she had just told the little girls, but he seemed undisturbed by her words and was or pretended to be calm.

The little girls obeyed Tanya. They returned the rest of the candies they held in their hands, turned around, took their jackets that were laying on the ground next to the slide and left the park.

Tanya turned around and faced Uncle Filip. She had waited this moment for so long and knew that sooner or later it would come. She was not anymore the little girl who was afraid and hopeless.

She was a grown-up woman, fearless and eager to bring this old pervert to justice. She knew it would be hard to do that, to prove that this old man who looked so innocent and fragile was a twisted man with a dirty mind. But she would do whatever was necessary.

"Listen to me, you, old pervert! You might look above suspicion, and maybe many people don't know what your real face is but I know and I can talk and put you in jail! Maybe you manage to trick other people showing them your false face and pretending that you are just an ordinary old man, but you are not! And you know it! And I don't want to waste my time on you, you, old scumbag, I just want to warn you. If I ever see you or hear that you are anywhere close to children, I will report you to the police and then, you will spend the last years of your life rotting in a prison cell or asylum. Or what is even better, you might get a bullet in your head by some aggravated parent."

Tanya was so angry and full of some dangerous spite that she felt like hitting Uncle Filip, or even beating him up, but she managed to come to her senses. Uncle Filip just remained standing there, with a blank look on his face, expressionless, as if he had slipped into deep meditation. Tanya's irritation by his calmness couldn't be hidden, but she was sickened by the fact that she had to face him, so she couldn't bear to look at him anymore. She turned around and left the park.

Tanya didn't want to give up on trying to stop this old pervert of doing something bad to children.

And even though pretty old, he was probably capable of traumatizing children the same way he had inflicted the shock upon her a long time ago.

The next few days, she walked through the park, sat for hours on the bench close to the playground, watched children playing, but she didn't see Uncle Filip again.

She spent the whole summer looking attentively around the town for Uncle Filip as if she had been afraid that without her doing that he would hurt some child. She thought that her pursuit of him was a certain way of guarding the children in her hometown.

At the end of summer, she reluctantly packed her things and went back to the university in the capital. Some strange fear and unease bothered her. It seemed to her that she had let all those children down. But she promised herself to come to her hometown more often. The town needed her. Particularly its children.

After two weeks, she went back home again. Her parents and grandparents were surprised but happy that she missed her boring hometown, but they didn't know the real reason of her coming back often. After she left her backpack at her house, and chatted for a while with her mother, she went to visit her grandparents.

Her grandma was alone at home, and she told her that her grandpa had gone to the funeral of his old friend. Tanya didn't pay much attention to her grandma's talk, until her grandma mentioned Uncle Filip. Uncle Filip had passed away. Mentioning of Uncle Filip struck her like an arrow. And all her senses were sharpened while she digested what her grandma had just said. Uncle Filip was dead.

Death was not something that brought comfort and pleasure. But this particular death set her soul free. As if her soul had been caged all those years, and her nerves always on alert unable to get loose, and her body always tense. Uncle Filip's death meant freedom. Freedom for her and other children. Maybe there were some other perverts like him out there that she didn't know, but at least this one would not disturb children anymore.

She gazed absentmindedly at her grandma who was telling her something about the garden and everyday house chores, but she couldn't focus anymore on listening to what she was saying. Her mind was too confused and perplexed by the fact that she didn't have to worry about Uncle Filip and what he might do to other children anymore. Even the smile elbowed its way on her face and out of blue, she hugged her grandma and told her that she loved her. Her grandma was confused by this sudden burst of emotions, but she returned hugs and kissed Tanya's cheeks.

That day, a long-sought relief filled Tanya. No matter of the occasions that brought it, that relief felt great. And if for a moment she thought that Uncle Filip hadn't deserved peaceful death but suffering and torturing, she couldn't say for sure that his troubled thoughts hadn't agonized them. At least she hoped so.

Days and months, and years went by, and Tanya, freed from the burden that she had carried as a little girl and teenager, realized how amazing it was to be free. Free from imprisonment, torturing, emotional pain, bad feelings. There was no price for freedom. It was precious. The secret that she had kept and which had bothered her for so long had never been revealed but instead it had been buried with the death of Uncle Filip. She was free of it and happy.

IT'S A KIND OF MAGIC

A Blue Finch

I keep many secrets in the pit of my stomach. My trees and shrubs witnessed many fortunate and unfortunate events that occurred in the depth of my body. And I helped many wretched souls that got lost among my thick tree trunks. On the other hand, I couldn't help to some of them. They were in a hopeless pursuit or running from their own wrongdoings. And their own deserved destiny caught them.

One lost soul especially got stuck in my memory. Her name was Hope.

Hope was a little blonde girl, not taller than my blueberry shrubs. She came to me breathing heavily, and almost losing breath. She was running like a wild animal pursued by the hunters. And she was pursued. She was pursued by strange people.

Those people were all dressed in black, and they carried the torches that lit their way. My body is dark and unwelcoming to those who have bad intentions. And seeing those people's eyes, I knew they meant evil to that little girl.

They yelled and laughed awfully, their voices harsh and scary. And their intention was to scare

Hope, make her stumble over some rock or tree trunk, fall down and get caught by them. For what reason they wanted to catch her, I didn't know, but I knew that they were not good people.

The terrified girl ran and kept losing balance, tired due to who knows how long running. Her pale face was wet, tears and sweat were mixing on it, and her blonde curls slicked down her back, wet and dirty. I opened my arms and took her. I hugged her and brought her to the deepest parts of myself. Those people couldn't find her there.

Hope entered the very dark area of the forest, and found a cave. It was pitch dark in the cave and in any other situation she would not dare to enter it, but this time, this cave was her savior. I knew that she would be safe there and I led her to the cave's entrance. She entered cautiously, sat on the dry ground, and tried to stabilize her heavy breathing.

Hope had some strange scars on her wrists, as if she had been shackled. Her legs and arms were all in bruises. I wondered who had been so cruel to this little girl. And how could have someone been so terrible to this innocent creature. Her doe-eyed face breathed with purity and her tiny body could not do harm to anyone or anything. Her frightened figure moved with her fast breathes and she cried silently trying to reduce any noise coming from her. I couldn't understand. But in the end, I never was able to understand humans. They tortured and killed for fun, they drank poison excessively, they ate when they were not hungry. What rule of nature did impose such a behavior? None. They were not the creatures of nature.

Hope was frightened. Her body trembled and she prayed to die peacefully without being like her mother and her father. She couldn't understand why her family was doomed to die in a terrible way, stoned, tortured and condemned. Why were they accused of witchcraft? And what the witchcraft was, anyway?

My heart was full seeing that Hope was getting better with every day that went by. I opened my secret places full of strawberries for her, and I led her to the stream to drink fresh water. Those people couldn't find her here.

But since autumn would come soon and cold winter would follow after, I started being worried how this little creature would survive the cold and lack of food. She didn't have fur to keep her warm, and she couldn't hibernate. She was too small to hunt wild animals and sooner or later she would become their prey. My heart ached when I thought that this poor creature would die alone. And I decided what to do.

It was getting colder with every new autumn day. And Hope's clothes were getting ripped off. And she didn't have any other clothing. She was worried. What would she do?

When the last days of autumn came and the cold northern wind started blowing carrying snow on its back, I opened my ground, still warm and cozy, and showed little Hope the underground labyrinth that the cold winter storms couldn't reach. Its catacombs were protected and only swallows and night gales lived there during winter. The green moss spread all around and formed a beautiful bed, comfortable and welcoming.

Hope entered the labyrinth and smiled. Her face bloomed with happiness and fear disappeared. She loved it there. There were always raspberries, and strawberries, and blueberries, no matter of the season. And the bird song entertained her. The birds taught her how to sing and by the end of winter, she sang better than most of them. Her old clothes were ragged since she had worn it for so long, though. And she walked half-naked.

I was sad to see Hope in those rags. Therefore, I gave her beautiful blue feathers and wings, and a yellow beak.

Once spring arrived, I opened the door of my labyrinth and let her out. First, Hope spread her wings insecurely, uncertain what to do and how to use them. But soon enough, after few trials, she spread soared in the air. I was happy.

Hope looked at her blue feathery clothing and wings and realized that she could fly. And wasn't it the most beautiful thing: to be free and to be able to fly?

Not long after, Hope found her friends, other blue finches, the rarest birds in my forests. And she joined them. They were all orphans, once upon a time, lost and miserable, who had looked for a shelter in the depths of my body. And I helped them. I gave them the shelter and brought them to one better world, the world of nature.

And if you come sometimes to my depths and look around carefully and noiselessly, you will spot a couple of them, jumping from one branch to another, soaring gracefully and singing the most beautiful songs you can imagine.

The Wild Red Rose

Maya loved the wild red rose next to her window. Her grandma often complained about its thorns and threatened to cut it but she never did. She liked it too, just didn't want to admit that.

Maya rarely left her room, except when she was supposed to see that tall man with a goatee and long white coat. He was a strange man. He pressed some cold device on her chest and asked her to open her mouth and protrude her tongue. She loved doing that, though. It was funny and made her smile. But she didn't like the needles that he sometimes left stuck in her arm and connected to some plastic bag full of water.

Those needles were the same like the thorns of her wild red rose. They were sharp and painful. She experienced both of them and somehow, she preferred her thorns. They were more familiar and homey.

She liked that man whose name she didn't know. Her grandma told her but she forgot it. She easily forgot things, especially names. She wished she could pronounce them. Maybe if she pronounced them, she would remember them. But unfortunately, she couldn't.

Her orientation in space and time was also bed. She rarely left her room, but when she did, and tried to explore the other rooms in her and her grandma's house, she got lost. All rooms seemed the same, and the only thing she remembered and never forgot was the wild red rose. That was what distinguished her room from the others. Often she would spend a lot of time entering the rooms and checking if the red rose was there outside the window touching gently the window pane. If she saw it, she was happy. It was like coming back home after hours spent in the deep forest without paths and indication marks.

Maya was really short. Only a meter and forty-eight centimeters. She looked like a kid and she felt like one. But they told her that she was a woman. Whatever it meant.

She didn't remember that she had ever had parents, even though, her grandma told her once that she had had them. Moreover, they had taken care of her when she was a baby before all of them had had a car accident. That car accident had taken them away from her and her grandma, and had left Maya with many defects. Maya didn't know what 'defects' were but she supposed it must have been something bad.

She had only one friend: her grandma. And she had never finished school. They sent her to the regular school and even some special schools where she had her own tutors but the progress was slow, almost non-existent. She had never learned to read or write.

Not many things kept her attention, either. Maybe birds and their song, and definitely her wild red rose. She loved watching this rose swaying in the wind. Its beautiful red flowers danced with even the lightest breeze and their movement gracefully filled the air. It was a beautiful scene that Maya watched every day sitting in her chair and staring through the window. This spectacle entertained her almost half a day. The rest of the day, she slept and dreamed the rose.

She often dreamed that she was the wild red rose, tall, graceful and beautiful. Her red layered dress swayed with the rhythm of bird song, and her red ballet shoes had a life of their own. They kept moving Maya around, elegantly going in circles and created the beautiful dance that only the best ballet dancers could perform. Maya could dance like that for hours and hours and once she got tired, she had to take them off, otherwise, they would continue its incessant dance without intention to stop. When she took them off, her dress fell off her body as well and slowly hanged itself on the hanger waiting for Maya to put her shoes on again. The shoes and the dress worked in unison. One without the other didn't function properly.

This recurring dream was the most beautiful thing Maya had ever experienced. And she looked forward to falling asleep, turning into the red wild rose and dancing gracefully with the wind, birds, sky and trees.

One winter, the town was covered in snow. Maya and her grandma's house got a heavy white coat.

The window was blurred and icy and through its frosted glass Maya saw the endless whiteness outside. Her wild red rose was freezing and Maya's grandma tried to it. She covered it with a dry soil and compost hoping that it would make a warm cover for the rose.

That winter Maya started feeling unwell. She couldn't walk anymore and she didn't feel like eating.

The food just didn't want to go down her throat. And her grandma took her again to that tall man with the funny goatee and long white coat. The man didn't smile much this time. He was unusually serious and his lips never formed the line that showed Maya that everything was all right. This time, something was not all right.

At the end of that winter, Maya dreamed her beautiful dream for the last time. That time, she managed to perform the most beautiful dance in front of not only birds and trees but her parents and grandma as well. She was so happy to see them smiling, clapping and cheering excitedly while admiring her dance. When she finished dancing, she bowed gracefully and they all gathered in a big hug. Maya smiled while dreaming.

The next morning, the grandma found Maya motionless and breathless with a big smile on her face.

Maya never woke up. The grandma's eyes filled with the tears and she remained sitting next to her granddaughter's bed holding her unmoving hand for hours.

That spring, the wild red rose didn't sprout. It had never woken up from its winter sleep. Or maybe and probably, it accompanied Maya in her adventure of endless dreaming and dancing. The two of them, in all likelihood, pursued the record of the longest dance.

A Yellow Marigold

A yellow marigold wanted to talk. She was just a garrulous little flower who couldn't keep silent. And she was so sad that other flowers didn't talk. They sometimes whispered some secrets to the wind that passed by and petted their yellow petals. But the little yellow marigold wanted to talk, seriously talk, sing, even shout loudly. However, she knew that if she started doing that, her petals would fall off and her green dress would disappear. And instead of a flower, she would become a little redhead girl who had no friends and whose home was not a happy place.

Maria lived in a shabby little house at the end of the village. The end of the road was the place where her father had built their home. And behind the house there was a beautiful forest that brought not only a fresh air and enchanting bird song, but the playground for Maria and her little sister Martha.

Their father was a miner and he often left the house and didn't come back for a week or two. He probably was trapped in those underground catacombs, as her mother had explained to Maria and Martha. And those days without him around were the best. Those days were filled with the peaceful hours, their mother's hands knitting, her soft voice singing, while Maria and Martha played in the garden. They didn't miss him, because he brought the awful alcohol odor, angry red eyes and his leather belt that left long red painful marks on Maria and her sister's skin. But those red marks didn't hurt as much as it hurt to watch him beating up their mother with his bare hands, fists and kicking her with his dirty boots. Those wounds hurt more. They left imperishable scars.

Every time her father came back stinking of beer, cigarettes and sweat, her mother would usher Maria and Martha to the forest and tell them to stay and play outside until she came to look for them.

They knew what would follow: their father's drunk yelling, throwing the chairs and other furniture around the house, and beating their mother. And they couldn't help her. They looked at her sad and terrified eyes and begged her to let them stay in the house with her. But she was persistent. They were to go immediately and play outside. The girls obediently did what their mother had asked them.

Once they went deeper in the forest and found those clean grassy areas with marigolds, strawberries, clovers and other colorful flowers, they forgot what might be happening in the house.

They got immersed in their playing and singing. Sometimes, they played for hours and hours before their mother came to find them. And the sight of their mother was terrifying. Even though she tried to mask her bruises, cuts and broken teeth, the little girls could see that she must have been in hell during those few hours. And they knew that coming back from that hell was announced only when their father fell asleep.

Every time they spotted their mother coming though the breeches and oak trees and looking for them, they rushed toward her carrying in their hands marigolds which they had picked up for her.

They hugged her and stayed long in her arms letting their mother's tears fall down on their hair and wetting their red curls. The three of them stayed embraced like that for a long time as if they hadn't seen one another for years.

Every time their mother sent them to play in the forest and they went to their favorite playground, Maria's heart ached with fear that their mother might not come to look for them that day. That thought made her panic. She was afraid to go back home alone with Martha, without their mother holding their hands and encouraging them to follow her back home. But they were also afraid to stay in the forest during the night. Night brought some strange sounds, shadows and creatures that lurked around and threatened to eat alive her and her sister. Night in forest was scary for little girls.

However, night at home while their father was there was not less frightening.

One gloomy day, when the sun hid behind the clouds and didn't want to show up, and the dark clouds covered the sky threatening to turn day into night, their mother with the tears in her eyes sent Maria and Martha to play in the forest. It was not a good day for playing outdoors, but their father was so drunk and angry that they could hear his scary voice a mile away.

Maria took Martha's hand and told her that everything would be fine. They walked slowly toward the forest which seemed dark and hostile. Their little hearts were beating fast but they comforted each other. They had one another. They were not alone. When they came close to the meadow full of marigolds, the thunder and lightning ripped the sky. Big rain drops started falling and, in a few minutes, Maria and Martha were wet. They looked around searching for a shelter but there was no cave, no place that could give them temporary protection from bad weather and danger. Maria took off her jacket and put it on the top of the blueberry bushes and then she and Marta hid below. At least the rain drops didn't fall directly on their heads but instead Maria's jacket collected them. They waited probably a couple of hours the rain to stop and when it finally stopped, they felt relieved.

But the sun didn't come out and since they were wet, they felt cold. They waited their mother to come and take them home.

Hours and hours passed and their mother didn't appear. The evening sky told them that maybe they would have to spend that night in the forest. Hungry and shaking due to being cold, they hugged each other and prayed.

When the darkness ruled over the forest and the temperature dropped significantly they fell asleep.

After some time, their breaths slowed down, and their hearts started beating less intensely until they completely stopped. And Maria and Martha fell into a deep eternal sleep.

The next morning, a hunter accompanied by his dog, found two little dresses, two pairs of old children's shoes, two little jackets and purple hair ribbons. But he didn't see any girls whom these things belonged. He and his dog searched the whole forest looking for the children but they didn't find them.

What the hunter and his dog didn't see were two beautiful yellow marigolds that stayed calmly and silently next to the place where the hunter had found the children's clothes.

Maria was restless in her new clothing and role of a flower. She admired her own gracefulness and fragrance, but she couldn't keep quiet. And she knew that every time she tried to talk, she would become a girl, vulnerable and lonely. Her sister Martha was happy, on the other hand, just to sit quietly and admire surroundings. She was safe and her sister Maria was next to her. And what was even more important, very soon, within a few weeks, their mother who had become a fairy, would come to look for them and take them with her. That's what the blue finch had told them. Their mother had sent him to inform her daughters that she hadn't abandoned them. But they had to be patient and silent and they should refrain from talking, otherwise, their father might find them and then, they would probably never again see their mother, who couldn't get back to her human figure.

Between death and life as a fairy, she chose the latter.

And now Maria and Martha were waiting. At least they didn't have to run away and hide. Here, no one disturbed them as long as they kept quiet. Talking and singing provoked Maria but the fact that if she kept quiet she would see her mother made Maria hushed. Just few more weeks. And then, the three of them, their mother, Martha and Maria will sing, smile and laugh altogether.

A Butterfly

Butterflies are not supposed to talk. Yes, I know that. But I am not an ordinary butterfly. My parents were hippies led by the idea that we could change this world and make it a better place. They believed in peace, love and freedom. And they lived the life they wanted. No constraints, no social injustice, no racism, no hatred, no criminal, no violence, no corruption. Those were some of their ideals.

I was born one cold February day in the small apartment which my parents inherited from my mother's grandma. It was a natural home birth, as my mother used to say. There was a labor nurse, a woman called Sonya, who helped my mother bring me to this world. But other than that, my mother did all by herself and she was proud of it. She used to say that I had appeared in the wondrous process that resembled the one of a caterpillar turning into a beautiful butterfly. Sonya became my godmother and our friend. And she named me Mariposa which means "butterfly" in Spanish.I was the only Mariposa in our town, and I was proud of it. I carried my name gracefully like a butterfly.

When I was very little, my parents even made me butterfly wings that I wore on my back while dancing happily.

My parents taught me to respect and appreciate everything I had and got and to be grateful for food, clothes, toys and other things they provided me with. And I did. I folded neatly my clothes and kept all clean clothing pieces in my small wooden closet. There were many old and faded jeans, T-shirts and skirts, but they were always so lovely arranged and they smelled nicely that no one would notice their shabbiness even when I wore them. They were clean and I wore them elegantly.

If there were some holes in those clothing pieces, my mum's magic hands made them disappear.

Moth holes in my wool sweaters were so sad, but my mother patched those holes with embroidered butterflies and my sweaters looked jolly again. She used some beautiful embroidery patterns to mend the patches and torn parts and no one ever guessed that those butterflies, frogs, rabbits, flowers on my jeans, sweaters, skirts, T-shirts and dresses were necessity. Somehow, they seemed natural and original parts of my clothes.

However, there was a war that our country led against some other far-away country that we didn't know much about. My parents and many other their friends protested against this war, against killing people, against sending our countrymen to kill other people. My parents took part in every protest, every demonstration against these killings. They marched, held the signs against the war, yelled and sang. And many many other people did the same. During those protests I stayed at home with Sonya and, sometimes, her daughter who was a baby in that time. The three of us played and watched TV and didn't go out during those dangerous hours that brought turmoil, a lot of policemen all around the town and some suspense in the air.

I didn't know much about anything what happened in the world, and I couldn't understand. But I knew my parents protested for a good cause.

In my innocence and incapability to understand the grown-up issues, I pretended I was a butterfly, a blue morpho. I put my wings on my back and I danced around the room. The sparkling blue and black wings carried me over the hills, meadows and forests into the unknown and exotic places, where people swam in the rivers and lived with the wild animals. I watched them and smiled. A couple of times, I flied over their heads and if I noticed that they were friendly and liked butterflies, I landed on their shoulders and arms and made them smile. Children loved me particularly. They ran after me and smiled. And they spread their arms pretending they were butterflies as well. I wanted to tell them that they could be if they really wanted to.

I was the blue morpho, one of the most beautiful butterflies in the world. The colors of my wings allowed me to make camouflage and I hid from predators, and sometimes, if I noticed the big lizards and birds coming toward me, I released the strong smell that chased them away. But I loved people. They were almost always happy to see me. Almost always.

Once, I spread my wings and flew over the unknown exotic, tropical and warm forests. The humidity made my wings heavy and I descended among the shrubs. I waited there and dried my wings on the sun. Then, I heard some strange noise, as if some explosions had been approaching me. But I didn't know what those explosions were about. I saw people running, among them scared children. Their faces were petrified, they were scared and panicking, and they ran away in front of people with big guns and rifles. Those people who carried the heavy weapons were angry. They were shouting madly, screaming some non-comprehendible words and shooting the people who ran away. I saw children falling down on the ground, as well as their parents. They fell and never stood up again. The blood covered the leaves and soil and the noise exploded through the forest. I was scared.

The people with guns kept coming and shooting and some of them came too close to me. Out of blue, some strange thing started flying toward me. It was not an animal, it was not a living thing, but it could fly faster and more ferocious than anything I had even seen flying. And all of a sudden, it hit me. My wings went all in pieces through the shrubs, the sparkling blue and black filled the air, and I looked at my own body exploding in the most magnificent colors. I didn't know what was going on, but I knew that I, the butterfly, the blue morpho, was dying. And then I just stopped breathing. And my butterfly body disappeared in the void.

When I opened my eyes, I saw that I was lying in my bed. My butterfly wings were broken and Sonya was sitting next to my bed. Her eyes were full of tears and she held the wet handkerchief in her hands and wept slowly. He sobbing voice hurt my heart.

"What happened, Sonya?" I asked with a feeble voice.

"You fell down the stairs, my dear child, when you heard the bad news." She said cautiously. And she turned her eyes to the other side as if fearing to face my eyes. I wanted my brain to work better.

I wanted to remember what the bad news were but I seemed so numbed and fragile.

"Your butterfly wings were damaged, my little Mariposa, but we will make the new ones." She started sobbing loudly again.

I looked around and remembered how I had died as a butterfly. But what had happened? And what the bad news was? I was scared to ask Sonya.

I tried to stand up from my bed and walk, but it seemed that my leg was broken. And seeing my effort to raise my body, she grabbed me in her arms, held me close to her chest and carried me to the living room.

All around the living room there were candles, and their burning warmed the entire room. I looked around and saw the photos of my parents displayed on the shelves and table. The flowers were everywhere as well, and the mix of the smells made the air suffocating. My heart started beating fast.

Sonya noticed my anxiety and confusion and she held me even harder to her chest.

"It is all right, my dear child. They are now in some better place. And those awful men with the guns who had killed them will be brought to justice. They would be sentenced and left to rot in some stinky cells condemned by the whole world."

And then, everything came back to me. The memory of the bad news brought by the neighbors and my shock and terror, and my falling down the stairs

My parents were shot during one of the protests; they were shot by the policemen, the men who were supposed to help people.

And what about all those ideals my parents had and embedded in me? Well, I don't know.

Somehow, when they died, those ideals crashed for some time as well. But I am trying to bring them back.

Sonya made me new butterfly wings. I am again the blue morpho. And that blue morpho flies gracefully over people's heads, makes them smile and laugh, and run after her. That butterfly tries to bring her own faith in people back and in the ideals that once were, as her parents taught her, the most precious things. The blue morpho sees the hope in children's eyes and believes optimistically that she and others would make those ideals become reality.

Mermaids

Mermaids were swimming in the shallow water, hoping that no human eye would notice them. But humans are canny creatures and their senses are sharp. They spot and smell and feel more than anyone knows. They hide wolves in their blood and sharks in their veins and scorpions in their eyes. The humans went hunting mermaids.

The mermaids were imprisoned, their wrists in shackles. Their freedom flew away and their eyes lost their color. Their tails became dry and their scales fell off.

Soon enough, their tails split into pairs of legs and they could walk on land. But it felt like walking on knives.

They tried to run away in the depths of the ocean when all the human guards were asleep. But the ocean threw them away. Their lungs were full of air and they couldn't breathe underwater anymore.

What were they now? Half-mermaids? Half-humans? Who did they belong to? Humans? The ocean? They were lost, lost between two worlds.

One world was their original home full of love, song, peace and water. And the other one was a scary place where they, for the first time, heard about malice, envy, hatred, jealousy, The feelings so scary that they couldn't believe someone was able to have them.

They cried and cried until they had no more tears left. They wandered in the wilderness and prayed to the Ocean God. But he didn't seem to hear them.

A deep forest was the only place which resembled the ocean. They could listen to the song of birds.

It was peaceful and green. And they had one another.

If you ever decide to go to the deep forest to look for the mermaids, go alone. And go with your heart. Fill your body with peace and love and hum your favorite song. If you are lucky enough, you will be able to see the shadows of mermaids.

About the Author

Ana Vidosavljevic from Serbia currently living in Indonesia. She has her work published or forthcoming in Down in the Dirt (Scar Publications), Literary Yard, RYL (Refresh Your Life), The Caterpillar, The Curlew, Eskimo Pie, Coldnoon, Perspectives, Indiana Voice Journal, The Raven Chronicles, Setu Bilingual Journal, Foliate Oak Literary Magazine, Quail Bell Magazine, Madcap Review, The Bookends Review, Gimmick Press, (mac)ro(mic), Scarlet Leaf Review. She worked on a GIEE 2011 project: Gender and Interdisciplinary Education for Engineers 2011 as a member of the Institute Mihailo Pupin team. She also attended the International Conference "Bullying and Abuse of Power" in November, 2010, in Prague, Czech Republic, where she presented her paper: "Cultural intolerance".